RESISTING ARREST

Fargo was on page three of the newspaper, reading an article about the Indian wars in Oklahoma Territory, when a knock came on the door.

And at the same time, a fat face appeared in the second-story window of Fargo's room. The window went up at the same time the door was opened with a skeleton key. Two men with sawed-off shotguns and badges came at him at the same time.

The fat one said, "You've been a bad boy, Mr. Fargo."

"You need to lose some weight. You're out of breath from climbing that fire escape."

The skinny one said, "We heard you were a joker."

The fat one said, "Old Harvey's gonna have a good time with this one. You can bet on that."

Both of them smelled of smoke and whiskey and sweat.

"Put the cuffs on him, Charlie," the skinny one said.

Fargo said, "No cuffs."

And that was when Charlie took the back of Fargo's head off with the butt edge of his sawed-off.

No need for cuffs now.

THE TRAILSMAN
#311

IDAHO IMPACT

by

Jon Sharpe

A SIGNET BOOK

SIGNET
Published by New American Library, a division of
Penguin Group (USA) Inc., 375 Hudson Street,
New York, New York 10014, USA
Penguin Group (Canada), 90 Eglinton Avenue East, Suite 700, Toronto,
Ontario M4P 2Y3, Canada (a division of Pearson Penguin Canada Inc.)
Penguin Books Ltd., 80 Strand, London WC2R 0RL, England
Penguin Ireland, 25 St. Stephen's Green, Dublin 2,
Ireland (a division of Penguin Books Ltd.)
Penguin Group (Australia), 250 Camberwell Road, Camberwell, Victoria 3124,
Australia (a division of Pearson Australia Group Pty. Ltd.)
Penguin Books India Pvt. Ltd., 11 Community Centre, Panchsheel Park,
New Delhi - 110 017, India
Penguin Group (NZ), 67 Apollo Drive, Rosedale, North Shore 0745,
Auckland, New Zealand (a division of Pearson New Zealand Ltd.)
Penguin Books (South Africa) (Pty.) Ltd., 24 Sturdee Avenue,
Rosebank, Johannesburg 2196, South Africa

Penguin Books Ltd., Registered Offices:
80 Strand, London WC2R 0RL, England

First published by Signet, an imprint of New American Library,
a division of Penguin Group (USA) Inc.

First Printing, September 2007
10 9 8 7 6 5 4 3 2 1

The first chapter of this book previously appeared in *Alaskan Vengeance*, the
three hundred tenth volume in this series.

Copyright © Penguin Group (USA) Inc., 2007
All rights reserved

 REGISTERED TRADEMARK—MARCA REGISTRADA

Printed in the United States of America

The Trailsman

Beginnings . . . they bend the tree and they mark the man. Skye Fargo was born when he was eighteen. Terror was his midwife, vengeance his first cry. Killing spawned Skye Fargo, ruthless, cold-blooded murder. Out of the acrid smoke of gunpowder still hanging in the air, he rose, cried out a promise never forgotten.

The Trailsman they began to call him all across the West: searcher, scout, hunter, the man who could see where others only looked, his skills for hire but not his soul, the man who lived each day to the fullest, yet trailed each tomorrow. Skye Fargo, the Trailsman, the seeker who could take the wildness of a land and the wanting of a woman and make them his own.

Idaho Territory, 1860—
a town of secrets, a town of violence is
dangerous to the man seeking the truth.

1

Skye Fargo, pitching his poker hand into the middle of the table, said, "I'm out."

"Hey, Fargo," laughed the slicker in the red vest and handlebar mustache, "you can't quit. I'm makin' too much money off you."

Fargo frowned. "I wouldn't push it, mister."

"Guess he don't know who you are, Mr. Fargo," said the old-timer sitting to the left of Fargo. To the slicker, he said, "I wouldn't be gloatin', mister. This one, he don't suffer fools."

Fargo stood up. "I'm the fool here. Havin' a bad night and should've quit about an hour ago."

"I didn't mean anything by that," the slicker said. "I was just havin' a little fun with ya was all."

"Already forgotten," Fargo said. "You boys finish up your game. I'm going to stand guard over those bottles behind the bar."

The crowd in the Gold Mine saloon had thinned out as ten p.m. approached. The sheriff of Twin Forks wanted to keep his town peaceful. He figured that drunks were at their worst as the hour drew later. He wanted the streets empty by the time he turned the jail over to his deputy for the night.

Fargo was riding through on his way to Boise, where he was to meet an old friend who was having problems with rustlers. The friend had learned that the range detective who'd been hired to keep the man's cattle safe was actually part of the rustling gang. Fargo would lend a hand and a gun if necessary.

Two beers and a shot of whiskey later, Fargo yawned,

1

looking forward to the hotel room he planned to take for the night. He'd played cards a couple of towns back and won decent money. He still had half of it left, even after the drubbing he'd taken this evening. He'd spent too many nights outdoors on the cold, hard autumn ground. He was rewarding himself.

He was just draining the last of his beer when the batwings opened behind him and the beefy Swede behind the bar said, "Not in here, miss. No ladies allowed."

"Whores would be all right, though, I'll bet."

Whoever she was, she had a mouth on her sharp as a bowie knife. Fargo just had to turn around and see what she looked like.

She was damned pretty, a sweet, slim little blonde all innocent of face, though the splendor of her curves defied the innocence of the eyes and mouth. She wore a blue Western shirt stuffed into a pair of denims that were, in turn, stuffed into a pair of Texas boots. But for all her good looks, the most notable thing about her was the .45 she carried in her right hand.

"I'm looking for a man named Theo Mason," she said.

"The banker from Redburn?"

"That's the one."

"He was in earlier. You can probably find him at his hotel."

"Appreciate it."

The Swede glanced at Fargo, then back at the girl. "What's the gun for?"

"The gun is for none of your business."

"You got a smart mouth on you for somebody your age."

She laughed. "So I hear." She seemed to notice Fargo for the first time. "You from town here?"

"Passing through."

"Thought so. You look too smart to be a yokel like the rest of these fellas."

The Swede said, "Good thing you're a gal. Otherwise you'd be walkin' around with a couple black eyes. You don't go insultin' my town without fightin' me—I'll tell you that."

But she'd left her deep blue eyes on Fargo. "Maybe we'll meet up later. My name's Bonnie McLure."

Fargo shrugged.

The girl disappeared between the batwings.

"Now there's a handful," Fargo said.

The Swede grinned, wiped massive hands on his dirty white apron. "In more ways than one. You see those tits of hers?"

"Yeah, I guess I did happen to notice them once or twice."

"And a nice bottom, too. But you'd have to put up with that mouth of hers." He poured himself a shot and threw it down. "Wonder what she wants Theo Mason for."

"My guess is, she wants to shoot him."

"That'd be my guess, too." The Swede called out to a man sitting at a table by himself. "Henry, get your ass over to the Hotel Royale. Ask for a Theo Mason. Tell him there's some gal lookin' for him. With a gun."

Henry, whose dusty clothes and ragged beard marked him as one of the many gold-crazed miners who'd come out here seeking a fortune, said, "You stand me to two drinks if I do?"

"I'll stand you to one."

"Two."

The Swede sighed. "You see the kind of crap I have to put up with, mister?"

Fargo smiled.

"Two drinks and I'll do it, Swede," Henry said.

"Two drinks it is," the Swede said amiably. "Now get going."

Fargo put his hat on, hitched up his gun belt and threw his saddlebags over his shoulder. Wind raced into the saloon, rattling the batwings. Nice night for a warm room with a warm bed.

He gave a little salute off the edge of his hat brim and walked outside. The town seemed respectful of the sheriff's curfew. A lone buggy was the only vehicle in sight. The other two saloons were already dark. Fargo headed west. That was where the hotels were located. The Excelsior promised the lowest rates. He didn't need a palace.

He thought of checking on his big Ovaro stallion. Sort of reassuring the animal that he hadn't deserted him. But the horse would be fine at the livery where he'd left him.

3

*   *   *

It was meant to be a scream but something muffled it.

Fargo was passing the mouth of an alley just as snow-flakes began appearing with no warning at all. He was just huddling deeper into his jacket when the sound came from the moon-shadowed alley.

He stopped, peered into the darkness. At first he saw nothing but a few garbage cans and a couple of stray cats sniffing around a back porch for food.

The silhouette of the man became coupled with the silhouette of the woman as he dragged her from behind a small loading dock. The dark shape of the woman was easy enough to recognize. She was the girl in the saloon who'd been looking for the banker.

The man slapped her with enough force to knock her to her knees. Then he reached down and grabbed her by the hair and yanked her to her feet again. The second blow was even harder than the first. This time her scream came loud and clear.

So much for my nice warm bed, Fargo thought. At least for now.

He dumped his saddlebags on the street and started running into the narrow alleyway. He pulled his Colt from its holster as he increased his speed.

By the time he reached the pair, the girl was on her knees again and the man was about to slap her.

Fargo was there in time to grab the man's wrist with enough fury to damn near snap it in half. The man groaned and tried to grab on to Fargo with his free hand. But Fargo was too quick. His fist hit the man squarely on the jaw. The man fell over backward.

Fargo tended to the girl. He helped her up. "You all right?"

"He's no gentleman."

"What the hell's going on here, anyway?"

"Do you have to swear?"

Fargo smiled. "You come into a saloon where no la-dies are allowed. You have a gun and you get smart-mouthed with the bartender. I guess I didn't figure you for having such delicate ears."

"I hate vulgarity."

"What happened to your gun?"

4

"I took it away from her," said the man who was just now getting to his feet. "Otherwise she would have killed me with it." He grasped his jaw with long fingers. "You could do all right for yourself in a boxing ring."

The man surprised Fargo. No anger in his voice, no anger on his moon-traced face. He even put his hand out. They shook. "I'm Theo Mason. This little hellcat is Bonnie McLure. We're having a disagreement."

"A lot more than a 'disagreement.'"

"I'm sure this man doesn't want to hear about our personal problems." To Fargo he said, "I shouldn't have hit her. But I got mad when she pulled the gun on me. I always get mad when I'm scared. I thought she was actually going to shoot me."

"I was going to, too, Theo."

Moonlight glinted off the .45 that lay next to the small loading dock. Fargo went over and picked it up. Looked to be the same gun she'd been toting in the saloon.

"I don't usually hit women."

"You sound like you deserve a medal."

Mason laughed. Though he was a dude in a three-piece suit, a boiled white shirt and a tan cravat to match the brown of his attire, there was a muscularity in his face and body that marked him as capable of defending himself. A lot of drunks had probably underestimated him, to their later dismay.

"You look like a man with a sense of humor. A medal for not hitting a woman. Did you hear that, Bonnie?"

"Yeah. Real funny."

Fargo looked from one to the other. "So am I through here?"

"He cheated on me."

"I'm too much of a gentleman to share some of her sins in public, Mr.—?"

"Fargo."

"Fargo it is. Her father raised her to be a lady, but you can see that it didn't quite work out that way." Mason was mad now and had been ever since she'd brought up his cheating. Fargo figured Mason was right. None of this was Fargo's business. In fact, it was embarrassing to stand here and have to hear it.

He looked wistfully to the head of the alley. He just

wanted to pick up his saddlebags and mosey over to the hotel.

"If you two try to kill each other later on, please leave me out of it, all right?"

Bonnie frowned. Mason laughed. "I'd feel the same way, Fargo. The same way exactly."

This was the first time Fargo had run into them together.

Unfortunately for him, it wouldn't be the last.

By the time he got to his hotel, Fargo was restless again. He found another card game in a room off the hotel taproom and sat in. No better luck this time than earlier in the evening.

After a couple of hands, one of the older players said, "No way I'm lettin' that little gal sit in again."

"She shouldn't be allowed in here anyway," another said.

"I still say the only way she won was she cheated," a third offered.

"Cheated and used those nice sweet breasts of hers."

"Not to mention those big blue eyes."

By now, the men were laughing.

"She take you for a lot of money?" Fargo said.

"She sure did, mister."

"But we deserved it. We were watchin' her instead of our cards."

"Exactly what did she look like?" Fargo asked.

And, just as expected, the description he got fit perfectly the young woman he'd seen in the alley with Theo Mason. He'd seen Mason strike the girl but the girl didn't seem hurt. In fact, there was a feeling of ritual to the whole thing, as if this happened to the two of them many times over.

"You know her?" one of the players asked.

"Met her briefly."

"She's an eyeful, ain't she?"

"I'll give her that," Fargo said. "She's an eyeful, all right."

"She take you for any money?"

Fargo laughed. "She didn't have the time. Otherwise, she'd probably have my horse and saddle by now."

"Women like her are a menace to society," said the first man. "They always get their way by cheating."

"That's 'cause we're stupid enough to let 'em," said the second.

"They never get hanged, either," said the third man. "Knew a gal over to Denver. Opened up her husband's throat with a butcher knife while he was sleepin'. And what did she serve for it? Three years. Judge and jury said her old man didn't treat her right. Made her real nervous all the time, see, what with his temper and whatnot. So she served three years and they let her go. And guess what."

"What?" said the first man.

"Couple years later she got herself another man and did the same damned thing all over again."

"Cut his throat?" the second man said.

"Ear to ear," said the storyteller.

"How much time did she serve for the second one?" the first man wanted to know.

"Take a guess," the storyteller said.

"Ten years?"

"Nope."

"Twenty?"

"Nope. Four years."

"Four years for doin' it a second time?"

Fargo pitched his cards and stood up. The boys were now more interested in talking than playing. But he'd learned one thing. That the young woman he'd seen in the alley was sure some piece of work—slick, slippery and probably dangerous as all hell.

2

Fargo's plan to sleep in was spoiled by a sharp series of knocks just after dawn. An irritating series of knocks. Did the caller have to be so damned loud?

Fargo jammed his pants on, grabbed his Colt and went to answer the door. He was all set to curse the caller until his eyes fell on the outsized sheriff's badge that rode on the man's heavy black jacket.

"You Fargo?"

"That's right."

"I'm Sheriff Dalquist."

"I noticed the badge."

"You don't sound happy to see me."

"I was hopin' to get some sleep."

"So was I. I'm not due into the office for another two hours. But my deputy thought I'd better handle this one myself." Dalquist was a ruddy-faced man the size of a mature bear. Perfect for throwing drunks around on busy weekend nights. "Get your clothes on."

"Why?"

"Why? Number one, because I'm the sheriff, and when I order you to do something, you'd damned well better do it. And number two, because I need your help identifying somebody."

"Afraid I can't be much help. I'm just passing through. I don't know anybody here so I wouldn't be much help identifying anybody."

"That ain't the way I heard it. Now get dressed."

Fargo cursed under his breath. He was starting to wake up. Getting back to sleep would be tough. Dalquist had ruined his sleeping-in plans. The bastard.

"I guess I might as well. You ruined my sleep anyway."

"Button the lip and get into those clothes."

Fargo was tempted to slug him. The problem with that idea was that he'd then find himself in jail, and in jail it was hard, what with all the drunks and punks, to get any sleep at all.

"Just a minute."

Fargo slammed the door in the lawman's face. He'd finish dressing without an audience.

"What's wrong with her?" Fargo asked the doctor.

This was a five-bed hospital on the ground floor of a large Victorian-style home. Dr. V. K. Holmes lived upstairs. With his Vandyke beard, his English-cut dark suit and his pince-nez eyeglasses, his personal style fit the style of the house very well. Holmes, who appeared to be in his fifties, apparently wanted to live in London. This was as close as he could get.

"I'm not sure," Holmes said. "Aside from the obvious, I mean."

The obvious being the bruised area and small cut on the right temple of Bonnie McLure's pretty little head.

Fargo had expected a corpse. That was the only kind of body identifying he'd ever done. But from the way her breasts rose and fell with her breathing, and the way her eyelids fluttered open from time to time, it was obvious she was alive.

For instance, now.

She stared up at Fargo, but there was no sign of recognition in her gaze. As if she'd never seen him before.

"Do you know her name?" the doctor asked.

"I know the name she gave me."

"Just answer his question," Dalquist said. "No funny business."

"As I said," Fargo said to the doctor, disregarding the lawman entirely, "the name she gave me was Bonnie McLure. But you never know these days. People use false names all the time."

"Maybe your name isn't really Skye Fargo," Dalquist said.

"Yeah. And maybe yours isn't really 'asshole.' "

"Gentlemen, for God's sake, I have a patient here. This is a hospital, or at least the only thing that passes for a hospital in this little burg of ours. Now please show some respect."

Fargo felt properly reprimanded. He and Dalquist should keep their obvious dislike for each other away from poor Bonnie, who'd apparently been seriously injured, from what the doctor said.

"Are you gentlemen familiar with the word 'amnesia'?"

"I certainly am," Dalquist said. "I ran into it several years ago. Had a prisoner who faked having it right up to the time we hung him."

Fargo repressed a smile. Dalquist mentioned the hanging with pride in his voice. In towns like these, such minor matters as evidence and proof didn't count for much when you had a sheriff—and a judge who went along with the sheriff—in control of the whole legal process.

"I think it's all fake," Dalquist said.

"I'm afraid I'll have to disagree with you," the doctor said. "This young woman can't remember anything about herself. Not even her name. I found an envelope in her pocket addressed to her. That's the only way I knew it."

"She claims she don't have no memory?" Dalquist said.

"That's right, Sheriff. And that's why I called you both here. Somebody saw Fargo here breaking up some kind of argument between her and a banker named Theo Mason last night. So I was sure Fargo would recognize her. So what do you know about them, Fargo?"

The Trailsman looked down at the dozing woman. She seemed to slip in and out of sleep. "They had some kind of argument."

"Were you able to figure out what it was about?"

"Not exactly. It had something to do with Mason cheating on her. But I noticed Mason wore a wedding ring and she didn't. Maybe he's seeing her on the sly."

Fargo watched her face carefully as he spoke. "I guess maybe she's thinking he'll leave his wife or something. You know how young girls are when they get sweet-talked by older men. They believe all the lies and then end up bitter. That's because they're stupid."

He was insulting her on purpose. He wanted to see if she was really asleep or just faking it. If she was listening in, her face would show some kind of displeasure at the "stupid" remark.

But not even her eyelids fluttered. Her face remained a mask of sleep.

Maybe her amnesia was real, unlikely as it was.

"Can you think of anything else, Mr. Fargo?" the doctor asked.

"Just that Mason seemed embarrassed by it all."

"He damned well should be embarrassed," Dalquist said. "He's an important man in Redburn—one of the city fathers. If it ever got back to the respectable citizens there that he was seeing this little girl on the side—"

The doctor nodded. "Tell you what. Let's let her sleep. I've got a pot of coffee on in my waiting room. We can sit down out there and try and figure out what we're going to do about her."

The medical man walked to the door and opened it. Dalquist took a final look at Bonnie McLure and then walked out, spurs jangling, into the next room.

Just before he turned to follow the sheriff out the door, Fargo glanced down at Bonnie McLure.

He was thinking, *Poor girl, she's had a rough time of it*—

Which was when she opened her left eye for just a second and winked at him.

This whole damned amnesia thing was a sham!

3

There were four hotels in town. Theo Mason of course was staying at the best, the Hotel Royale.

The desk clerk wasn't going to give Fargo any help. It had to mean trouble. Fargo assured him otherwise.

"He's an old friend. I just want to say hello."

"He said he doesn't want to be disturbed."

"I just got in. You don't want me walking up and down the hall knocking on every door, do you? Be a lot easier if I had the room number."

The clerk, a swarthy man a foot taller than Fargo, shook his head. "I don't know. I mean, I can't stop you but I can run and get the sheriff."

No sheriff, Fargo decided. There would be too many questions. And Fargo had no answers. He was simply curious now. He'd twice been dragged into the lives of Mason and the girl. He wanted to see what was going on.

"You have kids?"

"Yessir, two of them."

"Well, here's a little something toward their next birthdays. How's that?"

More than whiskey, more even than women, money could be counted on to seal most deals.

"Well—"

"I just need the room number. Knocking on every door. Waking everybody up. By the time you got the sheriff over here, I'd have most of your guests walking around in a real bad mood."

"Well, I guess—"

"So what's the number?"

A deep sigh. "Two-oh-nine."

And 209 it was.

When Theo Mason opened the door, the Trailsman pushed his Colt in his face and backed him into the room.

"I don't have all that much money on me." He was in a silly nightshirt but confronted with a gun he was surprisingly cool. "And I have to say, you don't look like a robber."

"I'm not robbing you. I just want to know what the hell's going on between you and the girl."

"Why?"

"Because I got dragged into it again. The sheriff had me over to the doc's office. She was there claiming she had amnesia."

Mason brayed a laugh. "She always uses that." He sounded merry about it. "And she's damned good at it, too. She fools everybody. She even fooled me with it the first time. I really thought she had amnesia."

Fargo felt naive. "You mean she goes around pretending she can't remember anything?"

"She usually manages to hurt herself when she's had too much to drink. Tonight she tripped and fell and landed on the side of her head. I left her at the doctor's and took off so the doc wouldn't see me. Then the damned doc went and called the sheriff. Bonnie didn't want to get me or herself involved with the law so she faked her amnesia. I hope all you folks get a good laugh out of this."

The Trailsman was too weary to hear any more. He jammed his Colt into his holster, took three steps toward Mason and then knocked him flat with a right hand.

Standing over the man, he said, "Maybe you'll get a good laugh out of that, too."

Then he headed to his own hotel.

Sleet scratched at the window of Fargo's hotel room. The weather had turned gray and grim about noon so he had decided to stay over one more night. Hopefully, he'd get a full eight hours' sleep with no sheriff interrupting it.

He wouldn't remember what he was dreaming of. All he'd know for sure was that it involved at least two women and that he was sure enjoying himself.

Then came the knock on the door. His first response was no, it wasn't possible. His sleep couldn't be interrupted two nights in a row. That wouldn't be fair.

But the knocking was persistent, so much so that the women in his dream ran away. They were naked and not ready for company. Too bad Fargo couldn't remember exactly what they had all been doing together on that big bed of theirs.

Crawled from bed. Jerked on his trousers. Filled his hand with his Colt. And went to the door, hoping he'd get to pump somebody full of lead. He deserved at least that much pleasure for being dragged from his dreams.

The flickering sconce light of the hall hid his visitor in shadow. He had to narrow his eyes to see her.

"What the hell're you doing here?" Fargo asked.

"Are you always this nice to your guests?"

"You're not a guest. You're a nuisance."

"Let me in. I've got an offer for you."

"I thought you had amnesia."

She smirked. "Well, that stupid doctor bought it. And so did the sheriff as far as I know. That way they left me alone."

Now he remembered what he didn't like about her. For all the innocence of her young face, there was always a suggestion of cynicism in her voice. Of manipulation. The same kind of cynicism and manipulation you heard in the voices of con artists all across the frontier. A part of them would always be laughing at you for being stupid enough to get sucked into their games.

"I'm going back to bed."

He closed the door on her.

She didn't wait long. He hadn't even reached the bed before she started pounding on the door. Up and down the hall he could hear people waking up and cursing.

She even started hammering with both fists instead of one. If he didn't open up and let her in, the night clerk would be up here and throw his ass out.

He opened up, grabbed a handful of her blond hair

14

and yanked her inside with such force that she went caroming off the far wall.

"God," she whined, "you tore some of my hair out."

He couldn't care less about her hair. "Why the hell did you come up here?"

"Why don't you turn up the lamp?"

"Why don't you answer my question?"

"My head really hurts where you grabbed my hair."

He went over to the bed and got his makings. He sat down and rolled a cigarette.

"Can I have one of those?"

"No. Now get the hell out of here."

"You're not even going to listen to my offer?"

"Doesn't look like it, does it?"

She helped herself to the lone chair. "Somebody murdered my father. He was worth a lot of money and he had a lot of enemies. I need somebody to help me find out who killed him."

"You don't have any law in your town?"

"The marshal there is an old man and he does what all the rich people tell him to do."

"You're rich. Why won't he listen to you?"

"He'll listen to my brother but not to me. My father and I didn't always get along—he sure hated me seeing Theo—but I owe him this. I want to find out who really killed him."

Fargo said nothing. Just listened to the patter of the sleet on the window glass in the shifting shadows of the small room.

When she stood up, he figured that she'd finally decided she'd get nowhere with him.

He figured she was leaving.

What he didn't figure at all was that she was about to perform a striptease that would trap him in the jaws of his own lust.

"That won't do any good," he told her as she began to unbutton her blouse.

She smiled at him. "I guess we'll see about that, won't we?"

"Don't say I didn't warn you."

She didn't acknowledge him in any way. She gave

herself up completely to whatever erotic fantasy was playing in her head. Her blouse fell away and in the dim light of the window he could see a pair of perfectly formed breasts, the nipples of which made his mouth water despite his pledge not to be moved by her striptease.

She tweaked her nipples until they were hard and erect. Until she began breathing in small gasps that only got louder as her hands slowly made their way to her jeans, which she dragged down past her hips. The musky smell of her made him dizzy with desire. He had to force himself to sit still. He wanted to grab on to her narrow but womanly hips and pull her to him.

Her gasps grew louder as she found her own erotic center and began to work it with a skillful finger.

She writhed as if in the middle of having sex with an invisible partner. And Fargo could hold off no longer.

He stood up and pulled her to him. The scent and feel of her tightened his crotch as the pull of desire overwhelmed him. He took her back with him as he fell on the bed. And then her mouth was on his and her hand was finding its way inside his pants, making acquaintance of the epic spear that yearned to plunge deep inside her. She nearly tore his pants off, freeing him of his burden. And then she moved her mouth from his face to his manhood. He groaned so loud he half expected the walls to collapse. She really knew what she was doing.

But he wanted to finish inside her. Nothing beat good old-fashioned missionary-position sex for the grand finale. He eased her away from his crotch and sat up so that she was riding his rod while she sat on his lap. He speared her again and again. Now it was her turn to knock the walls down. They were sure giving all the old coots who stayed in the Excelsior a thrill they hadn't experienced in a long time.

She clung to him, moving so that he could go deeper and deeper inside her, both their legs dripping with her pleasure. But before his turn at finality came, he eased her off him and onto the bed. He took her thin but shapely legs in his hands and put them on his shoulders.

Then he began driving even deeper than he had when she was sitting on his lap. This time they were both groaning at the same time—groaning and laughing at the noise they made.

When he reached the pinnacle, she slipped away from him so that she could once again find his crotch. She licked him the way she would a lollipop. Licked him with such zest that he was just about ready to go again.

But for now, they were both finished. They lay back, sweaty and drained, as she said, "I knew you'd be good, Fargo. But I didn't know you'd be *that* good."

"You're not bad yourself."

"Meaning I'm damned good and you just don't want to admit it." Then she jabbed him playfully in the ribs. "You just don't want to admit that I seduced you into breaking your word. You weren't going to sleep with me, remember?"

"Guess I must've forgot about that," he laughed.

Then he sat up and rolled them a cigarette that they shared.

With her head on his biceps, she said, "You have much money?"

"You thinking of robbing me?"

"No. I was thinking of giving you some."

"How much we talking about?"

"Oh," she said, "somewhere around twenty-five hundred. And I'll give you a third of it down if you'll help me."

"Why, hell, that would be about—"

She smiled at him. "I think I finally got you interested, Fargo."

Fargo had been innocent of real money for a long time now. A man needed greenbacks if he was to enjoy the finer things—women and wine and good meals. Not to mention nice plump beds at night when sleep was the finest pastime of all. He didn't trust her worth a damn but he figured he might as well find out what she was up to.

"Damned interested," he said.

17

4

As a haggler, little Miss Bonnie McLure was an embarrassment.

She needed a horse so they went behind the livery to where a rope corral housed an even dozen of equines for all. And for reasonable prices as far as Fargo could see. The trouble was Bonnie found something wrong with every one of them.

Sam, the livery owner, took to rolling his eyes every time she started her spiel about the problems with a particular horse. Too heavy, too lean, look at those flanks, look at that neck, is that some kind of skin disease, he looks like he's blind in one eye, what the heck makes him smell like that?

True, none of these fellows would ever be hired for stud service nor for a horse race. But since all she needed was horseflesh transportation to where the banker lived, any one of these boys would do fine.

Finally, she found one with what she said was "the least number of problems." She then proceeded to offer Sam exactly half of what his stated price was.

"No," he said. He was a stub of a man but explosive in the way of all people who'd spent their lives literally looking up to most of the people they met. "You know how long we've been at this?"

"Why should I care how long we've been at this? I'm the customer."

"One half hour is how long we've been at this. You know how long it usually takes a customer?"

"No. And I don't *care*, either."

"It usually takes them five to ten minutes. And they always pay the asking price."

"Good for them. But I *never* pay the asking price for anything."

Sam sighed. It was an epic sigh—one that embodied all the frustrations and heartbreak of a life lived on the margins. Liverymen didn't exactly get rich, not unless they had the rich people's trade, and in Sam's town that particular trade went to Malley's up the street. Malley had finished high school and was a Lutheran. The carriage trade saw him as one of their own.

Sam addressed Fargo. "Tell you what, Fargo. You I like. You're a reasonable man. Tell this woman if she takes the horse and the saddle I'll throw in for an extra eight dollars, I'll let her have the horse for her price. But she has to agree to never set foot on my property again."

Fargo laughed. "That sounds more than reasonable to me, Sam."

"Hey, Fargo, I can make my own deals."

Fargo said, "She'll take it, Sam."

"Just leave the money with the Negro man up front. I'm going to the saloon for a couple beers."

Fargo said, "I don't blame you one bit, Sam."

The train was late. As usual. Town marshal Harvey DeLong grabbed himself a folding chair, placed it on the depot platform, opened up his newspaper and proceeded to wait for the earth to rumble as the train neared the station.

He had to deliver bad news. Worse, he had to deliver bad news to somebody important. Unimportant people getting bad news—who gave a damn? Unimportant people never contributed to his reelection campaigns or even attended his rallies. He was the pawn of the rich and those voters the rich bullied into voting for him.

He just wished that the man about to get the terrible news wasn't right at the top of the list of important folks. Somewhere down the middle of the list would be better. Or near the bottom of the list. But no. He had to be right at the top now, didn't he?

He scanned the news stories. He always looked for

ones with sex in them. And if he couldn't find sex, then he held out for violence. And if he couldn't find sex or violence he went to greed—robbery or somebody coming into a gold strike or inheriting an unexpected fortune.

It was a hell of a poor day for news. There wasn't anything even close to sex, violence or greed.

He felt the earth begin to shake. Not much. You had to know how to feel it; most people didn't. There was a faint throbbing in the soles of his boots. Right up through the wood of the platform. The whole platform vibrated, in fact.

And as the train got closer, the vibration became more pronounced. It still thrilled him. He'd never get used to the childlike pleasure only a train could inspire in him. Faraway places. Mountains. Oceans. Exotic sights. It really did turn him into a kid again.

But then all the fun went out of the moment. He started thinking about important people again and how they didn't appreciate those who delivered bad news. Sometimes they got so crazy they blamed the messengers for the bad news, as if they'd had something to do with it.

All he could do was hope that this one particular person was a little bit more sensible than that.

David McLure stepped off the train and saw Harvey DeLong watching him. McLure, a rangy twenty-six-year-old in a gray three-piece suit and the type of dark derby now in favor with businessmen, smiled a greeting. But Harvey didn't return the smile. Usually he was a glad-hander with anybody he considered important, and in this town anybody with the name McLure was damned important. But now the bulky fifty-six-year-old looked somber as hell.

So McLure went up to him, a Denver newspaper tucked under one arm and his fishing gear and duffel bag under the other.

"Afternoon, Harvey."

"Afternoon, David." He was good about remembering how much David hated being called "Dave." Made him sound like a little boy, he always said. Not only didn't Harvey offer a backslap and a dirty joke today, he wouldn't even meet David's gaze.

"Something wrong, Harvey? And for God's sake, look at me, will you?"

"Oh, sorry." He gulped and raised his eyes. He looked miserable. "I've been trying to get hold of you for a week."

"I was fishing, Harvey. Out of contact. Everybody knew that. Now dammit, tell me what you're so upset about."

Harvey paused for a moment, obviously trying to think of the right way to impart his information. He apparently decided the best way was to just lay it out there straight. "Somebody murdered your father."

"What the hell are you talking about, Harvey?"

"I'm sorry I had to tell you that. I was hopin' somebody would get to you before I did. You know how much I respected your father."

McClure snapped, "Who killed him?"

"We arrested Seth Parker."

"Seth? That's impossible. He's one of the best ranch hands my father ever had."

"Not after he caught Seth stealing from him. Snuck into your house one night and stole some money out of your dad's desk. And your dad caught him and fired him. Seth went out and tied one on and came back the next night and slugged your old man. Couple of the other hands had to break it up."

"That doesn't prove he killed my father."

"Well, your dad was murdered the next night in his office and your maid, Beth, walked in on Seth sitting in a corner and crying with your old man dead in his desk chair. Two bullets in the chest. What else would you make of it? He sure sounds like the killer to me."

"Did he confess?"

Harvey snorted. "They never confess. Not right at first, anyway. He said he'd planned to ask your old man to forgive him and let him have his old job back."

"It just doesn't sound like Seth."

"Well, you're welcome to come and talk to him any time you'd like. He's sittin' in a cell. And he sure ain't going anywhere—I'll assure you of that. Now I better get back to the office." Then he stopped. "There's only one piece that don't fit yet."

"Goddammit, Harvey, tell me everything and tell me right now. I'm about ready to come apart here. My father was my best friend. I want to get the hell out of here and be alone."

"Seth wasn't wearing a gun. And we can't find the gun he used. We figured he musta tossed it somewhere outside."

McLure touched his fingers to his Navy Colt holstered on his right hip. "I'll tell you something, Harvey. If you can convince me Seth did it, you won't have to worry about any trial. I'll come right to your jail and shoot him in his cell. And that's a promise."

And with that, he brushed past the lawman with enough force to make DeLong move back a foot or so.

Damn, DeLong thought. He hadn't been lying to McLure. He'd really hoped that somebody else would have contacted David first and explained to him what had happened. You never wanted to put yourself in a position where you had to give important people bad news. Sometimes they blamed you as much as the culprit.

"I can see why you make so many friends," Fargo said as he rode alongside Bonnie McLure on their way to her hometown. The day was crisp and clear, signs of autumn just now setting in.

"I don't care about making friends. I care about not getting cheated. People think because my dad was rich that they can charge me higher prices."

"He offered you a fair price."

"Fair to him, maybe. Not to me. This is a nag, in case you hadn't noticed."

Fargo could see that arguing with her was pointless. She was relentless in pushing her version of the truth. She'd dropped all pretense of being the helpless girl she'd first presented herself as. That was her pose. This was her real self.

"I'm still not sure what we're going to do when we get there," Fargo said.

"Is it really that complicated? We're going to find out who killed my father."

"What if we can't figure out who it was?"

"Well, then we'll just go after whoever looks guilty to us."

"You ever hear of a thing called evidence?"

"Evidence can always be planted, Fargo. It's done all the time."

"Not by me."

"Oh, I forgot. You're true-blue all the way."

Fargo grabbed her shoulder. "I agreed to help you find out who killed your father. I can use the money and I'll admit it. But I won't have anything to do with setting somebody up. Either we get real evidence or I ride off with your down payment in my pocket. Are we clear on that?"

She mocked him. "Oh, yessir, Reverend Fargo. We'll do everything the Good Book tells us to. Does that satisfy you?"

But he'd learned his lesson by now. There was no way he was getting dragged into another argument with her. He rode on in silence.

5

Marshal Harvey DeLong knew it wasn't a good thing to be summoned to Theo Mason's office. A social visit, Theo would just stop in and bring along a couple of good cigars and have Harvey tell him some jail stories. Theo loved jail stories, prisoners misbehaving, especially fights, the bloodier the better. He also appreciated stories of how old Harve got confessions out of so many reluctant confessors. Some of those were the bloodiest of all.

But when Theo summoned Harvey to Theo's office at the bank . . . well, Theo wanted something and something big.

Harvey had all these thoughts as he made his way to the bank. He could look around, smiling and hat doffing and even kissing a baby or two, while all the time his mind was fixed on the pressures of the moment.

The bank employees all smiled at Harvey. He knew they'd voted against him in the last election. They were younger people and they saw Harvey as an old fool kept in office by the wealthy of this town—the very people they were here to serve.

Harvey was shown to the large office in the rear. Theo had had it designed by some Eastern fellow who spent four months out here. It was as much like a boardroom as an office, with a long oak table dividing the large room in half, an imposing mahogany desk in the right corner and mahogany wainscoting on every wall. The Western portraits were good, pioneer stock and all that. The exception was the somewhat ludicrous portrait of Theo himself. He was all got up in Western clothes with a six-shooter strapped to his hip inside a fancy holster, and he was looking up at the sky like some mythic hero. It was downright embarrassing, knowing that this was how Theo saw himself. It was like admitting to some vile sexual secret.

Theo had his stogie ready. He handed it to Harvey before Harvey was able to plant his considerable butt in a chair.

"Enjoy it, my friend. We're talking two dollars apiece."

"You sure know how to live, Theo."

"And I plan to keep on living this way for many years to come." He paused, giving Harvey time to notice the sheen of sweat on Theo's face. The man actually looked scared. "And with your help, I'll be able to keep on living the life I enjoy. And share with people like you."

Theo liked to hear himself talk. It usually took ten, fifteen minutes of blather before you could figure out what he wanted from you. Not today. Today he was coming right to the point.

"I sure want to help you any way I can."

"Fine, then. I'll tell you what I need. Hell, light up, man. You don't want to waste a two-dollar cigar."

He was looser now, more confident, now that he knew that Harvey would go along with him.

Harvey scratched a match across the sole of his boot and lighted the stogie. It damned sure was a two-dollar cigar. Sweet and smoky.

He waited for Theo Mason to speak.

"How sure are you of this Seth Parker being the killer?"

"Pretty damned sure."

"One hundred percent?"

"Maybe 98.9 percent. Why?"

"Because." Mason paused. "Because I'm afraid that Bonnie McLure's going to come back here and stir up trouble."

"I thought you got along with the McLures. Hell, you're their banker and their attorney." He paused. "And I realize you and Bonnie have a special relationship."

Theo said, "I want to move on Seth Parker as fast as we can."

"I've talked to the judge. He said he'll clear the docket for a crime like this. Speedy trial."

"And speedy hanging."

"Exactly."

Harvey frowned. "You afraid of the same thing I am?"

"I am, and you know I am. We've all got nice lives in this town. But a long investigation about McLure's death—no tellin' what might come out." He smiled. "You and I have taken some liberties with the law, Harvey. When we couldn't get our way, we had to bend the law books a bit. Same as old man McLure did. This is for the common good, Harvey. Let's just wrap it up."

Theo stood up, put hands on hips, stretched his back. "Not as young as I used to be, Harvey." He laughed sourly. "Can't even screw like I used to."

Whenever Theo stood up, the meeting was over. Harvey grappled to his feet—he really did need to take some of that weight off—and said, "My Mr. Charlie goes on strike every once in a while. I think I plumb wore him out back there in my youth."

Theo walked him to the door and said, "Remember, Harvey, we need to take care of Seth Parker right away."

Harvey cuffed Theo Mason on the arm. "Don't you worry, Theo. It's practically done already."

While Bonnie McLure rode off to her father's spread, Fargo found a livery, a saloon and finally a hotel.

He was just going up the steps of the King's Inn—but he had to wonder how many kings ever stayed in a two-story stuccoed abode like this one—when he saw a familiar face. And not a welcome one.

Theo Mason saw him at the same time.

Both men hesitated. Then Mason broke into a deeply insincere smile and approached Fargo, leading with a right hand meant for shaking.

"Well, I'm certainly glad I got the chance to apologize for our little misunderstanding the other night, Mr. Fargo."

He was treating the Trailsman like a preferred bank customer.

Fargo didn't take the offered hand.

"Don't tell me you're still mad. Hell, I'm apologizing. I'm taking the blame for it all."

"I should tell you that I'm here with Bonnie."

The smile vanished and so did the hand that had still been poised for a gentlemanly shake. "I see. Any reason why you came back here with her?"

"I said I'd help her find out who killed her father."

Mason beamed. "Well, what do you know? I'm happy to tell you that we know who killed McLure and we're expecting a speedy trial."

"That marshal of yours works fast."

"Experience. He knows what he's doing. Hell, Fargo, you could be riding out of here by tomorrow morning."

Fargo took stock of Mason. He liked him less and less. "Is that a threat?"

"Just a suggestion. They've arrested Seth Parker, a ranch hand, for the murder. I imagine you've got more exciting places to go than our little town." He paused, face and voice much harder now. "There's nothing here for you, Fargo."

"I guess I'll have to find that out for myself."

He picked up his saddlebags, threw them over his shoulder and walked up the steps of the hotel. He knew that Mason was still there, probably glaring at him now.

He was glad he could give the man some fear.

Fargo had just settled in when somebody knocked on his door. He'd been rolling a cigarette and looking forward to reading a Denver newspaper somebody had left behind. He groaned a bit at the interruption, pitched himself off the bed and walked in stockinged feet to the door.

A prim little man he recognized as the desk clerk said, "I'm sorry, Mr. Fargo. I'm afraid I have some bad news."

What the hell was this all about? Fargo wondered irritably. Bad news? He didn't know anybody in town except Bonnie and Theo Mason. And the clerk wouldn't be delivering bad news from them.

"Bad news?"

"I mistakenly gave you the wrong room."

"What the hell are you talking about?"

For the first time, the little man looked nervous. "I—this room was reserved and I forgot that. And now the couple who reserved it is downstairs."

"Give them another room."

"That's the problem. There *isn't* any other room. This is the last one we have to rent."

"So you expect me to leave?"

"I'm afraid there's no other choice. If you don't—Well, I'd probably lose my job. And I've got a sickly wife."

"Sure you do."

"I'm glad you understand."

Fargo gave him a little shove. "Oh, I understand, all right. I understand that Theo Mason told you to throw me out. Well, you tell him for me that he'll have to do it himself. Otherwise I'm not leaving."

The clerk looked pale. He leaned in confidentially. "Mr. Mason asked me personally to do this. He'll be terribly disappointed. And if there's one thing you don't want to do in this town, it's disappoint Mr. Mason."

Fargo sighed. "Look, I know you're getting pushed around here. And I'm sorry for that. But I'm staying."

"Oh, Lord, I don't know what to do now."

"Sorry," Fargo said and closed the door.

He was on page three of the newspaper, reading an article about the Indian wars in Oklahoma Territory, when another knock came on the door.

And at the same time, a face appeared in the second-story window of Fargo's room. The window went up at the same time the door was opened with a skeleton key. Two men with sawed-off shotguns and badges came at him at the same time.

The fat one said, "You've been a bad boy, Mr. Fargo."

"You need to lose some weight. You're out of breath from climbing that fire escape."

The skinny one said, "We heard you were a joker."

The fat one said, "Old Harvey's gonna have a good time with this one. You can bet on that."

Both of them smelled of smoke and whiskey and sweat.

"Put the cuffs on him, Charlie," the skinny one said.

Fargo said, "No cuffs."

And that was when Charlie took the back of Fargo's head off with the butt edge of his sawed-off.

No need for cuffs now.

They just dragged him down the fire escape, his toes stinging from hitting the metal rungs.

6

There had been a time when her father's ranch hands pretended to like young Miss Bonnie, as she'd then been called. But even the pretense was gone now.

Without knocking, she entered the bunkhouse and looked around for somebody to talk to. Nobody home. This was a workday and that was one thing the hands were proud of—their work.

But as she turned away from the two rows of cots and all the magazine pages on the walls—mostly of pretty Eastern women—she walked right into Biff McGivern, the foreman.

He immediately looked suspicious. "I help you with something?"

"You don't have to say that like I'm some kind of criminal."

But he didn't back down. "How do I know what you're doing in there?"

In the past two years, Bonnie had seduced two of his best cowpokes. She'd set them to fighting against each other over her. Finally, the younger one, in despair and shame, had left the ranch and headed for New Mexico. Her father and brother had been angry about it. But what could they do? When she got bored again, she'd probably find a new one to destroy.

"I want to know about Seth."

"What about Seth? According to Harvey DeLong, he killed your father."

"You don't believe that?"

"No, I don't. Seth'd never kill your dad. No matter how drunk he was."

"Then who did?"

McGivern was a muscular, red-haired man with a deep scar running from his left ear to the back of his left jaw. When he sneered, as now, he looked particularly ominous. "The marshal just wanted to arrest somebody quick-like, whether Seth was guilty or not."

"If he wasn't guilty, what was he doing in my father's office?"

"He might've been in there but that still don't mean he killed him."

"Then who did?"

His smile was as menacing as his sneer. "Why don't you ask the marshal that? Maybe he'll get off his dead ass and find the real killer."

He didn't wait for her to stand aside. He nudged her aside and went into the bunkhouse.

David McLure listened, which, as his wife, Sarah, was thinking, was remarkable. He seldom listened to her in any serious way. He just wanted a quick summary of what she wanted to say. And then he wanted to be gone. Hers was the world of the household—of problems with the maid, of problems with their two little girls, of problems with David's sister, Bonnie—and his was the world of men. Of money. Of power. Of manly prestige.

Today was different.

They'd been in the study now for more than an hour and he'd barely spoken. He'd simply let her words paint a portrait of his father's last days and in particular of his two arguments with Seth Parker, the ranch hand the old man had basically regarded as his second son.

"I'm sorry, honey. That was an awful lot for you to shoulder."

"You haven't always worried about how much I have to shoulder."

He flushed. Their love life had faded with the years. No doubt about that. David took her in his arms. "I'm sorry I'm not as frisky as I used to be."

"Well, neither am I, when it comes down to that. But this is nice. Just holding me like this. This way I feel less like your secretary."

"Oh, God, not the 'secretary' thing again."

"Well, that's how I feel sometimes."

"Fine. You were telling me that you heard Dad and Seth arguing."

"Yes. And from what I was able to hear, it was about the money that Seth took. I doubt that your dad cared about the money—it wasn't all that much—but he cared about Seth betraying him that way. That had to be hard for him."

"That was the first night they argued?"

"Yes."

"How about the second night?"

"I heard fighting. It woke me up. Then I heard Beth call for me. When I ran downstairs, I went to your father's office and I saw Beth at the door. She looked terrified. I went in past her and saw Seth in the corner. Crying."

McLure shook his head. "Seth—I just can't believe it."

"Neither can I. But I saw it. He was pretty drunk, too. He may not even remember much of it. Then a couple of the other hands came running in. They saw the same thing I did. And they couldn't believe it, either."

"And I had to be away. Fishing."

She slid her arm around him. "Well, you couldn't know. Nobody could."

She was just about to kiss him when she heard steps outside the study door. She turned to see her sister-in-law, Bonnie, there.

"Well, this is a cozy little scene," Bonnie said. "Looks like you two are all happy again." She delighted in their occasional arguments. It seemed to give her a sense of power over them.

McLure's stomach clutched. His sister's sarcasm was hard enough to deal with under normal circumstances. Under these—

"Don't even start, Bonnie. Dad's dead. We need to think about that and nothing else."

"Oh, yes, dear old Dad."

McLure had suspected it before. Now he was sure. His little sister was drinking again. "I thought you promised Dad you'd quit the drinking."

"You may not have noticed but dear old Dad isn't around anymore."

"That doesn't mean you have to run to the liquor cabinet right away."

Bonnie laughed. "You're such a priss, David. I don't know how poor Sarah here can put up with you, especially when she's got so many men eyeing her all the time. Everywhere she goes, they watch her. They're just waiting for the slightest invitation. And who knows, if you get any prissier, she may just take one of them up on it. Right, Sarah?"

"You're such a miserable woman, Bonnie," Sarah said. "I don't know how you can stand being yourself."

"On second thought, Sarah—maybe you're just as prissy as my brother is."

She smiled. And was gone.

The Trailsman had been hit just about every way possible during his years of wandering. Left hands, right hands, feet, heels, bats, pipes, clubs, blackjacks—they'd all been applied to his various body parts. But he couldn't remember a fist ever packing such force. Especially since it was being thrown by a fat old man with a stupid kid grin on his face. He was enjoying the hell out of himself.

And there wasn't a damned thing Fargo could do about it. He was roped to a chair in a back room of the jail, alone with town Marshal Harvey DeLong.

"Did you see me grin, mister?"

"Yeah, I sure did," Fargo said around a mouthful of blood. "And I'll be grinning when it's my turn."

Harvey looked surprised. "Now that was a dumb thing to say. And you know why?"

"Because you're gonna hit me again for sayin' it?" His words were barely understandable.

"That's right. You coulda just kept your trap shut and you woulda been fine. But you had to sound off."

He hit Fargo with a right hand this time. The chair went over backward and Fargo with it.

The lawman went over and righted the chair. Then he went over to another chair and sat down and lighted up a cheap cigar.

"We'd appreciate it if you'd leave town. That's what we were tryin' to suggest when my boys rousted you out

33

of your room. You couldn't be that dumb, could you? I mean, you had to know we're runnin' you out of town."

Fargo said nothing.

"So what I'm gonna do is let you get cleaned up here and then walk you over to the livery and you can get on your horse and ride out of town."

Fargo said nothing.

"Hell, boy, you were all talk a couple of minutes ago. You bite your tongue off, did you?"

"Theo Mason," Fargo said, articulating as well as he could given the blood pooling inside his mouth.

The lawman shook his head. "You really are that dumb, I guess, huh? You're going to tell me something bad about one of our leading citizens?"

"He's the one running me out. Not you."

"And just why would somebody as important as Mr. Mason be running somebody as unimportant as you out of town?"

"He thinks I can help Bonnie McLure."

The town marshal laughed. It was a deep and resonant laugh. "You mean you're hooked up with Bonnie? Son, that's a living hell you've walked into. Nobody gets out alive except Bonnie. She's brought more men to their grave than any war you can name. A lot of them are buried right outside the town limits, to the north, in case you want to see them. She loves turning men like you into knights. You know, like King Arthur's men. Rescuin' the damsel in distress and all that. She'll concoct some kind of story and then one of her beaus will go out to damage some fella she said hurt her or stole from her or insulted her—and then the man she sent out'll get himself shot or stabbed or beaten to death. And Bonnie won't care. She'll just go on to the next fool."

For some reason—and almost against his will—Fargo had the feeling that the lawman was telling him the truth. He'd sensed that kind of craziness in Bonnie. And now it had become clear.

The lawman surprised him. Came over and untied him. Helped him to his feet. "Right now, you're hating me, son. I had you all trussed up there and I hit you pretty hard. And you'd like to get a couple of quick pokes at me to pay me back. But hear me good. I just did you a favor. One hell of a favor, when you come right down to it. Because I warned you off a little gal who's nothing but trouble. I'd do the same thing to my own son if he told me he was gettin' mixed up with her. The very same thing."

He led Fargo out one door, down a hall and up to another door. "Now you go in there and get yourself cleaned up. I'll be up front in my office. You stop by on your way to the livery and tell me good-bye. I want to make sure that everything's going according to plan so I don't have to worry about it. I got enough headaches in this town, son, believe me."

Fargo swallowed blood. "What if I don't leave town?"

Harvey DeLong laughed. "Then you're a glutton for punishment, and that's a fact. Because if you don't leave town when the marshal tells you to—well, all sorts of things could happen to you. And if you think I mean death, that's absolutely right. Death is definitely one of those things. That's no threat. I'm not sayin' you *will* die, but I have t'tell you, that's within the realm of possibility. Very much within the realm of possibility, in fact. Now you get in there and get cleaned up."

Fargo spent fifteen minutes washing up, trying to rinse his mouth out so he could speak clearly, wringing the sweat out of his shirt. He needed a bath and fresh clothes. He also needed to whale on the town marshal for a good hour or two. Harvey seemed as crazy as everybody else he'd met here—Theo Mason, Bonnie and every clerk who seemed to be on the Theo Mason payroll.

Harvey DeLong was smoking a cigar when Fargo reached the front office. "Guess what I did, Mr. Fargo."

Fargo glared at him.

"I took the liberty of walking over to the livery and telling the man you'd be along any minute now. He's even going to have that nice big Ovaro all saddled up and everything for you. Now that's a neighborly thing to do, wouldn't you say?"

Fargo started toward the door.

"And you know something else, Mr. Fargo? I even paid your bill. Yep, you don't owe the livery a dime. You just go over there and get up in that saddle and head straight out of town. East or west. Your choice. Now that's another nice neighborly thing I done for you."

Fargo opened the door.

"I want you to have good memories of our town, Mr. Fargo. I surely do."

Fargo slammed the door before Harvey DeLong could say anything else.

7

Twenty minutes later, Fargo was in a saloon, enjoying a beer. His mouth had not been cut up as bad as he thought. He'd be damned if he'd be run out of this or any other town when he'd broken no laws. He also had vague plans about paying the gabby town marshal back for all the pain he'd inflicted on Fargo. And then Fargo would look up Theo Mason and put a lot of pain on him. He was the son of a bitch behind the beating. He'd obviously told DeLong to run Fargo out of town.

Fargo was just starting on beer number two when the tall, beefy man behind the bar said, "We ain't supposed to serve you."

"Who says?"

"One of the deputies. Reckon he hit all the saloons. Described you. Said if we served you, we'd be run into jail ourselves."

"So why did you serve me?"

The older man shrugged. "Too old to fight somebody like you. Though I got to say, you don't look so good right now. DeLong do that to you?"

"Yeah."

"One of his 'interrogations'?"

"I guess that's what he calls them."

"You're lucky."

"Right now," Fargo said, talking around his swollen mouth, "I don't feel so lucky."

"He's killed men in that little room of his."

"And nobody goes after him?"

"He knows who to butter up. He's got the judge and all the rich people in town on his side. If I was you, I'd

37

move on. Second time he gets you back there in that room of his, you could be in big trouble."

"I appreciate the advice. But right now I don't feel like moving on. I'm going back to my hotel room and get a little sleep in."

"Up to you, mister."

Fargo walked along the street, not noticing at first how many people stared at him. When he became aware of them, he smiled. This was some town. DeLong had certainly spread the word about him. Fargo was now officially a pariah.

His big Ovaro stallion waited for him outside the hotel. The horse was saddled and ready to go. All of Fargo's clothes had been jammed into his saddlebags. They really, really wanted to get rid of him, this town did.

As soon as the desk clerk saw him, he came rushing out. He kept a safe distance between himself and Fargo. "I packed those saddlebags as good as I could, Mr. Fargo. And I didn't steal one single thing from you. I want you to know that."

No point in disliking this man, Fargo knew. His life was here, probably had a family, a church, a men's club he belonged to, the Odd Fellows being very popular these days. And the price of enjoying these things into the future was going along with whatever DeLong told him to do.

"I appreciate that."

"This wasn't my idea."

"I know."

"I wouldn't want you mad at me."

The man was literally trembling.

"I'm not going to hurt you. Relax."

"I appreciate that, Mr. Fargo. Well"—he turned his head back to the interior of the hotel lobby—"I guess I'd better get back inside."

Fargo walked his horse down the street to the bank. He used the hitching post out front, cinched his saddlebags tighter, set his hat at an irritatingly jaunty angle, and then stepped up to the double doors that led inside.

He performed several doffings of the hat for elderly ladies, holding the door for them as well, and inside strode up to the teller cages with the air of a man who'd just struck gold. All he needed was a big cigar and a wad of greenbacks sticking out of his shirt pocket.

He knew that if he looked sullen and ready for trouble he'd never get to see Theo Mason. But with his swagger and his smile, the pinch-faced man in the teller cage said, "Well, you go straight back, sir. You'll see a desk there with a lady named Dorothy. She's sort of keeper of the gate. You just ask her to see Mr. Mason and I'm sure she'll escort you right in."

This had to be the only place the word hadn't been spread about him, Fargo figured. Nobody had seemed to recognize him.

He continued his plucky ways. He saw a vase of violets on one desk and stole them. Carried them back to where Dorothy, a flinty-eyed lady who could probably whip a bear bare-handed, watched in disbelief as he set the violets on her desk.

"Did these come from up front?" she asked.

"They certainly did not, ma'am. I bought them up the street and carried them in here myself."

Dorothy calmed down. "Well, for a minute there—"

"I'd like to see Mr. Mason if I might."

"Your name?"

"Devin McLure."

She looked at him more closely. "McLure? Of the local McLures?"

"I'm David and Bonnie's first cousin."

"I see." She was a bit confused now. If he was really blood kin to the McLures, she'd have to be an awful lot nicer than she'd been so far. But if he wasn't—

She erred on the side of keeping her job.

"I'll ask if he can see you now. Excuse me."

The Trailsman stood there grinning, still in a courtly frame of mind. She knocked twice sharply on a mahogany door and then stepped inside quickly. Fargo heard muffled words exchanged and then the door opened.

"Mr. McLure, won't you please step in?"

This was the trickiest part of all, Fargo knew. He had to get inside Mason's office with the door closed before Mason had a chance to recognize him.

"Thank you very much," Fargo said, moving quickly

around the side of her desk and doubling his speed as he approached Mason's office.

Then he was inside, closing the door. Mason was seated behind his desk, glancing through some papers. As he was looking up to see who'd entered his office, Fargo hit him with a roundhouse right that knocked Mason's reading glasses all the way across the room. He then proceeded to break Mason's nose and ruin a couple of teeth.

He wasn't finished. He grabbed Mason's coat lapels and picked the man up and hurled him into a glass-fronted bookcase. The glass shattered. Mason cried out. Fargo turned and said, "I owe you a hell of a lot more than that, Mason. Just be glad I don't have any more time to spend here today."

When he walked out of the office, he faced a wall of employees and customers.

They were all whispering and nodding in his direction. The men looked more frightened than the women, probably because they knew he wouldn't hit ladies but he sure would hit men. There was no hat-doffing this time. He was still angry that he hadn't had the opportunity to break a few of Theo Mason's bones. The nose wasn't good enough, not even with a couple of teeth thrown in.

His stallion still awaited him outside. He recalled from the ride into town a couple of cabins along the river that said BUNKS FOR RENT. He knew that staying within the town limits would only lead to jail. But DeLong hadn't said anything about sitting just outside those limits and sneaking into town when he needed to.

The cabin was cleaner than he expected. It was a sort of dirt-cheap hotel for travelers of the cowhand variety. You could take a bath in the river, cook a meal over a campfire and rest yourself on a pretty decent cot. The Trailsman wasn't one for enclosed spaces. He flipped a coin with another guy but lost. Fargo got the bottom bunk.

That night as he lay awake reviewing the past few days, he realized that he no longer cared about the money. While that had been the first attraction, what he wanted now was revenge. He didn't like being pushed around by people like Mason who hired their brutality done rather than doing it themselves.

There was another reason to stay, too. He wanted to know what the hell was going on between Mason and Bonnie. The only thing he knew for sure was that they'd both lied to him.

Unable to sleep, he went outside and sat by the dying campfire, rolling smokes and thinking things over. He was glad to be alone. Even from here he could hear the others snoring in the cabin. Kind of funny, the various noises they made. He was glad for the comic relief because when he thought of how Bonnie and this town had treated him right from the start, he wasn't happy at all. He was damned mad. Punching mad. Maybe even killing mad. That was the thought he dragged along with him as he went back inside and fell asleep. Bonnie and Mason and all their lies.

His dreams of vengeance made for good sleeping right up until dawn when somebody shoved a six-shooter in his face.

8

"You Fargo?"

"Yeah? What about it?"

"I'm supposed to give you a message."

"What message? And what the hell's the gun for?"

"The gun's for— She said you were dangerous."

"Who said?"

"Miss Bonnie."

"Good old Miss Bonnie."

"She wants you to meet her tonight at the boat dock near her old man's house."

Fargo was lying flat on his back. He hadn't moved. The cowpoke with the gun had been lulled into thinking that Fargo would just accept the gun pushed in his face.

But Fargo wasn't that kind. This was just one more indignity he had suffered from this town. Lawmen, bankers, rich citizens and now cowhands were all ready and eager to pound, beat and threaten him.

When Fargo rolled off the bed, he did so with speed and accuracy. He grabbed the cowpoke around the knees and brought him down, then threw him on the bed while he snatched the six-shooter from the cowpoke's hand.

The cowpoke lay flat on his back on Fargo's bed.

As the other men started to wake up from the commotion, Fargo pushed the six-shooter in the man's face. Then he slapped him hard enough to raise a welt on the skinny man's cheek. "Never point a gun at me unless you're going to kill me."

"I was just scared, mister. I didn't even want to deliver

the message. But Miss Bonnie said to get the drop on you before you got it on me. I was just protecting myself, mister, honest."

"What time am I supposed to meet her?"

"Around eight o'clock, she said."

"Tell her I'll be there."

He reached down and grabbed the man by the top of his red-and-black flannel shirt. "And tell her never to send a man after me with a gun. Not unless she plans to see him in a funeral home."

"I told ya. I didn't want to come here in the first place. But you know how Miss Bonnie is."

Fargo smiled coldly. "I'm beginning to find out, anyway."

Five minutes later, he jumped in the river with a bar of soap and went about washing up. The water was cool and made him feel not only clean but purposeful. He was damned well going to find out what Miss Bonnie wanted. And then he was going to get the truth from her.

He had the same thought again—the same thought over and over again—*She's using me, but why?*

"I'm sorry you had to miss the funeral," Sarah McLure said. She and David were having breakfast in the library. The mullioned windows overlooked the rolling green of the backyard. The trees and grass were a virtual aviary. So many kinds of birds that even Sarah, who spent hours reading about and identifying birds, had no idea about some of them. Her latest mystery involved a robinlike creature that had a feathery hat of purple. For all the colors of their plumage, Sarah had never seen purple feathers before.

"So am I."

"We tried to find you."

"I know. That's what Harvey told me."

"Harvey." She nearly spat the name.

"He isn't so bad."

"Not if you're one of the chosen."

David sighed. "Isn't it a little early in the day for your political speeches?"

"He's the worst kind of bully, David, and you know it. He hides behind his badge so that nobody can touch him."

David smirked. "And he doesn't believe that women should have the right to vote. And he doesn't support the government giving food to poor people. And he doesn't think that teachers who believe in socialism have any place in our schools—"

"You're just making fun of me."

He reached across the table and touched her long, elegant hand. "I'm not making fun of you, Sarah. It's just that you get so angry with people who disagree with you where politics are concerned."

"I just want to see your face when women get the vote. You won't be so sarcastic then."

"You know my feelings on that. Women and men have different interests. Women should stay home and—"

"Not worry their pretty little heads about politics. They should take care of the children and supervise the maids and make sure that everything is just wonderful around the house so that when the lord and master gets home, he can relax and enjoy himself."

"I do work hard, Sarah."

"See. You don't like sarcasm, either. I just hurt your feelings. Like you hurt mine every time you take that attitude about me and politics. It doesn't feel very good, does it?"

David said, "What's going on out there?"

Bonnie and her sometime fiancé, Glen Davis, had been walking across the backyard when they suddenly stopped, turned and faced each other. And then Bonnie had struck him openhanded with such force that Glen had been knocked on his heels.

David's opinion of the two was that they deserved each other. Rich, vain, spoiled, they were useless in David's eyes. Both just waiting around for portions of the family fortunes to be squandered on them. David's father was dead now. Glen's soon would be. The doc said that his heart wouldn't last much longer.

Their arguing was the only thing that David found interesting about the two. They argued everywhere.

Once they'd gotten into a row in the back of church. Most of the parishioners found the doings in back much more urgent than the doings in front. They'd turned around and watched the drama play out.

Today, there was an added surprise.

Glen, a slender blond man with sun-streaked hair and an impudently handsome face, slapped her right back.

Hard.

She, too, was rocked on her heels.

"What the hell's going on out there?" David snapped. "You better stop them."

He was out the door and across the back lawn in moments. When he reached them, she was patting the jaw he'd struck her on.

He came up behind Davis, grabbed his shoulder, spun him around and hit him with a left uppercut that knocked the man out before he even hit the ground.

"Did you have to hit him that hard?"

"Well, it was either that or let him hit you again."

"He thought I cheated on him."

"Was he right?"

She smiled. Her bitch smile. How he hated her bitch smile. "Your sweet little sister cheat on her fiancé? What do you think?"

"I don't know who's more disgusting," David said, forgetting about his sister and his protective feelings toward her. Her bitch smile reminded him of everything he loathed about her. Everything their father had loathed about her. "You or Davis."

"Oh, probably me. He's still got a little bit of his innocence left. I don't. I'm just as ruthless as our poor old daddy was."

"Don't talk about our father that way. You know I hate that."

She shook her head. "You're the innocent one, David. You could never admit to yourself that our father was a ruthless old man who crushed anybody who got in his way. That's why it was always so funny when he condemned me—he was really condemning himself. I grew up being just like him—you grew up being just like Mom."

He blushed. He hated hearing that, even though he

45

knew it was true. He'd once heard the ranch hands make the joke, "Bonnie is the son the old man never had." Meaning of course that David didn't have the guts or the gall of his old man. But Bonnie sure did.

Davis had regained consciousness. Bonnie was tending to him. "Next time you want to hit me, make sure my big brother isn't around anywhere. He thinks he's defending the family honor."

"I ever hear of you hitting or slapping her again, Davis, I'll come after you. And I'll do a lot more than knock you out, believe me."

Davis just looked baffled. He wanted to say that he was surprised that big brother would defend a sister he so obviously disapproved of. But he was still so dizzy from the punch that he wasn't sure he could speak clearly. He was also afraid that he might get hit again.

"You'd better remember what I say, Davis."

And with that, David stalked away.

The long arm of the law, Fargo thought, as he saw one of Harvey DeLong's deputies approach the cabin where Fargo had spent the night.

Fargo stood in front of the cabin, hand on his gun. He hoped that this would warn the deputy away from trying anything foolish. He didn't remember the older man's name but he did recall the face. The man had been in and out of the room where DeLong had inflicted the beating on Fargo.

"No need for that," the deputy said, stepping down from his horse. "I didn't come for no shoot-out."

As he walked toward Fargo, the gray-haired man wiped a sheen of sweat from his forehead with the sleeve of his shirt. He had a middle-aged face that had seen its share of fights and hadn't done especially well by any of them. Maybe he was one of those men who just enjoyed fighting and it didn't matter if he won or lost.

"DeLong just wanted me to ride out here and remind you of something."

"Yeah? What was that?"

"That he knows what you're up to."

"And what would that be?"

"That you'll stay here but sneak into town."

"He's a genius, your boss."

"He just wanted me to give you the message that if he catches you in town, you're going to spend more time in his little room."

"I notice you were in and out of there a lot."

The older man looked uncomfortable. "He don't like my attitude, I guess."

"About what?"

"About—you know, the beatings he gives people. I don't much have the stomach for them. Slapping people around a little bit don't bother me. But what DeLong does . . . but he's the town marshal. He can pretty much do what he wants."

"He makes you watch?"

"He tries. But I can never stay longer than a few minutes. You got to have the nerve for seein' something like that. I always end up feeling sorry for the man being beat. Even murderers can get to me sometimes. That's why I always leave. If I ever said anything, old Harvey would put *me* in the chair."

"You really think so?"

"Old Harvey? Are you kidding? He'd put his mother in that chair if he was mad enough." He hesitated. "So I'd be careful. I'm gonna tell him you told me you wouldn't come into town."

"Tell him whatever you want. That won't stop me."

"I'm tryin' to help you, mister. When Harvey puts you in the chair a second time—well, let's just say that a few men never survived it."

"And nobody complains?"

"Who would complain? The men he kills are drifters and bums. They got nobody who'd complain for them. He's careful. He never kills a man who's got any kin in town. He came close once but the fella made it through after about three weeks in a coma. You can believe me or not, mister. I'm giving you the same advice I'd give anybody. Don't give Harvey a crack at you a second time. And in your case that means don't sneak into town."

He wasn't a bad sort, Fargo decided. "Well, I appreciate the advice. I guess we'll both have to see how this plays out."

A sadness crept into the man's blue eyes. "Yes, I guess we will."

An autumn dusk made the food at the campfire taste better than usual, the hot food a pleasant contrast to the cold weather.

Ordinarily, Fargo would have joined in the various conversations but he was preoccupied with his coming visit with Bonnie McLure. By this time, his distrust of her was at the point where he considered her capable of about anything. He'd had to deal with treachery most of his life but he'd never met anyone who seemed to delight in lying to people as much as she did.

He took his time riding out to the McLure spread. He wore his sheepskin with the collar up. He enjoyed looking at the stars on a clear, chill night like this. He had half a mind to just keep on riding. The whole town had become a kind of hell for him. No friends, not much money, and the chance that the town marshal might throw him in a cell and forget all about him.

But when he saw the spread, and the mansion lit up the way it would be on New Year's Eve, he felt the excitement of the moment. Bonnie wasn't much of a lady but she sure as hell kept you guessing.

A melancholy violin solo pierced the frosty night. Somebody in that house knew the instrument well.

He rode east, swinging around the spread itself, to the river that he could smell from here. His first glimpse filled him with memories of his boyhood. A thin silver skin of ice had already formed on the water. A little sturdier ice would mean ice skating, a pastime he'd enjoyed many times as a youth.

Bonnie couldn't have known that the night would be so cold. She might have chosen somewhere warmer than the dock for a meeting.

From here he could see three rowboats and a small utility cargo boat tied to the dock. The boathouse on shore was the size of most home garages where horses and buggies were kept. The wood-shingled roof glowed with frost that looked like fur in the moonlight.

He dismounted on the path above the dock and walked down. For good measure he slipped his Colt from his holster. With Bonnie, he reminded himself, you could never be sure what you were walking into.

When he reached the shore, he stood on the dock for a few minutes, taking in the scent of the land and water. Somehow the stars seemed even brighter now.

He wondered if Bonnie was watching him from the boathouse. As he walked toward it, he could smell grease and oil. Vessels were repaired inside. Locals took this waterway seriously. It was a busy river for shipping from Idaho Territory to states and territories below. Vessels had to be in good shape to compete with the railroads. Both land and water businesses were thriving.

The boathouse looked darker than it had a few minutes ago. The door was ajar. The lone front window was like looking into a bottomless well. He could see nothing but darkness, not even a hint of light from the moon.

Maybe she was late.

Or maybe, given Bonnie's nature, she'd decided not to show up at all.

Or maybe she'd lured him into some kind of trap.

With Bonnie, it was impossible to know.

He decided to go inside. The barrel of his Colt led the way. He pushed aside the partly open door and took two steps across the threshold. Pitiless darkness, though the stink of oil and grease was stronger than ever.

He bumped into a rowboat that was up on wooden sawhorses. And when he turned around to look for a clear path, he nudged a small table on which he heard a familiar sound. The chimney of a lantern rattling against its metal base.

He took out a lucifer and struck it against his gun belt. The match flare was almost blinding in darkness this deep. But he'd been right. There on the table was a lantern. He quickly found the wick and set it to burning. Lantern in hand, he started a full tour of the small place.

So she really had shown after all, he thought when he saw her. He almost felt guilty for thinking so ill of her.

Her killer had put one bullet in her forehead and one above her right breast. She looked ghostly in the dirty yellow lantern light, a creature out of Edgar Allan Poe.

No, he thought, she hadn't been much of a lady, but did she really have this coming to her?

9

Over the course of the next few hours, what had been an isolated, quiet area became a noisy, crowded public site. Half the people carried lanterns. A few carried torches. They came on horseback, buggy, bicycle. They came from farms, adjoining spreads, town. The youngest looked to be six or seven; the oldest used an ear horn, a cane and had a wooden wheelchair standing by just in case the cane wasn't sufficient.

Town marshal Harvey DeLong was unhappy with all the people. He had already interviewed the Trailsman once, not to mention slapping him around. He had also done a couple of cursory interviews with David McLure and his wife, Sarah. The problem was that no matter where he went to interview them, there were always gawkers somewhere near trying to hear every word.

With an election coming up, though, DeLong had to be cordial. This time, he needed every vote he could get. He knew that he was considered old and corrupt and his methods out of date. People, the bastards, read newspapers these days. All crime news referred to the talents of Scotland Yard and how big-city American police forces were solving crimes by emulating the ways of the Yard. The Yard happened to bore DeLong's ass off, even though when asked about it—and some of the things the Pinkertons were doing, too—he always said that he and his staff of fine deputies were studying the ways of the Yard and about to implement them Any Day now.

Fargo sat in one of the rowboats that was tied to the

dock. He rolled a few smokes and watched as DeLong tried to do his work. Judging by the irritation in his voice, DeLong could go another five, six minutes before exploding and ordering everybody not directly connected with the murder off the McLure spread.

Fargo watched as Theo Mason approached the rowboat. He'd seen Mason earlier. Given the kind of combustible relationship Mason had had with Bonnie, Mason was likely a suspect in the case.

Tonight, Mason wasn't dressed fancy. He wore a sheepskin, jeans and boots that came to about midcalf. He carried a Winchester. He got stopped a couple of times on his way to the rowboat. As an important man, his opinion was sought out by poor people who reasoned that you had to be smart to have as much money as Mr. Mason had. So Mason gave his opinion that poor Bonnie had been murdered, most likely, by some old beau she'd cast aside. You know how old beaus get sometimes, he noted. They get so worked up over being cast aside that they go crazy. Literally crazy. And do things they'd normally never think of doing. He then cited two examples of beaus who'd killed their ex-fiancées. Maybe this was no different.

Fargo was amused by how seriously and solemnly Mason's audience took him. Moses wouldn't have gotten such a reception.

When he was done orating, Mason came down to the dock and walked over to where Fargo sat in the rowboat.

Mason smiled. "Permission to come aboard, sir?" He gave a jaunty little grin despite the nose Fargo had recently broken.

"I can hear you fine from up there."

"Did you kill her, Fargo? That's all I want to know."

"No, I didn't. Did you?"

"Me? Why would I kill her?"

"You two had a lot of battles."

"Battles are one thing—murder is quite another, and it's a good thing I know you're being sarcastic. Otherwise I'd—"

"Otherwise you'd what?"

Realizing what he'd started to say, Mason quickly said, "All I meant was that I'm glad you don't really think I killed her."

"You're as good a suspect as any."

"So are you."

As he spoke, Fargo looked beyond Mason and saw DeLong and David McLure coming down the steep embankment that led to the dock. DeLong toted a sawed-off shotgun now. Mason turned to watch them, too.

DeLong was swaggering a bit. The sawed-off seemed to make him feel younger and tougher. McLure didn't have a shotgun but he looked angry as hell.

"Somebody told me you boys left," DeLong said after he'd walked onto the dock. "A good thing they were wrong."

"I don't like your tone there, Harvey."

"Just doing my duty, Theo. Nothing to get concerned about. But both you fellas knew her and have seen her recently." Deference had started to seep into his tone. He didn't back down completely but he'd obviously realized that he'd been a little tough when he first stepped onto the dock. Theo Mason was, after all, Theo Mason. And in this town, that mattered.

David McLure said, "I'm not afraid of you the way Harvey is, Theo. I never approved of you hanging around my sister. You're supposed to be married. Or maybe you think that's all right. Maybe that's the kind of world you want to live in, where marriage vows don't matter."

"I say this kindly, David. You should've been a preacher. You've always been so high-and-mighty. And you got the voice for it. All you need is a Bible to wave in the air."

"This isn't funny, Mason. Somebody murdered my sister and I'm sure we'll find out it had something to do with the kind of life she led. She knew way too many people like you."

"You going to talk to me again or can I go?" Fargo said to the lawman. "I'm sorry she's dead. I don't know why she wanted me to come out here. And I don't know who killed her. Same things I told you earlier."

"I still want to talk to you tomorrow."

Fargo smiled. "So now you want me to stay in town, huh? Yesterday you told me to leave."

"I'm glad you find this funny, Fargo. Nobody else does."

Fargo stood up in the rowboat, hoisted himself up on the dock. "I don't think it's funny she died, DeLong. I just think it's funny that you don't seem to know what the hell you're doing."

"And I suppose you do?"

"Well, every once in a while I read the newspapers. And they're always talking about how Scotland Yard and the Pinkertons handle what they call 'the crime scene.' From what I saw, you didn't spend any time having your deputies go over the boathouse up there. You might have found all kinds of things the killer accidentally left behind. But you let so many people in there to look around, we'll never know now who belongs to what."

"That stuff's all bull. I've handled more murder cases than anybody I know."

"And I'll bet you probably hanged a good share of innocent people while you were at it because you didn't know how to look for evidence."

As he spoke, he noticed that McLure's expression had changed from anger to interest.

"Is it too late to go back over the boathouse, Fargo?"

"Probably. But I'd still give it a try."

"You sound like you know what you're talking about. Would you help me search the place?"

"This isn't my fight, McLure. Sorry."

McLure was angry again. "You knew her. Maybe even intimately. You don't think you could show her a little honor by trying to find her killer?"

"If anybody finds her killer, it's gonna be me," DeLong said.

"Yeah, and you're doing such a damned good job of it, Harvey," McLure said. Then: "C'mon, Fargo. Pitch in. You, too, Mason." He smirked. "And you can join in, too, Harvey, if you'd like to. We'll all get lanterns and go over that boathouse inch by inch. Maybe we'll get lucky. And then tomorrow when it's daylight, Harvey can get a couple of his deputies to go over it again."

Fargo was thinking of having a couple of beers and getting a room in town for the night. He wouldn't say no to a good meal, either. But McLure was good at putting shame on a man—he did indeed have the makings of a preacher—and so now Fargo felt obliged to join in the search.

"Well, I guess those beers'll still be there later on," he said. "We might as well get going on the boathouse."

"I appreciate this, Fargo."

"Just go easy on the sermons, McLure. I got enough of those when I was growing up."

Any other time, McLure probably would have smarted at Fargo's sarcastic words. But it was obvious his only concern now was finding the person who'd killed his sister.

As if he'd suddenly taken charge by unanimous consent, Harvey DeLong said, "I'm gonna deputize you men right here and now for this search. That means I'm the boss and you do what I say. You got that?"

Fargo said, "This gets worse all the time."

"You watch your mouth there, Deputy."

The four of them climbed the embankment to the boathouse.

By the time the boathouse search was finished, only a few people remained down on the dock. The night had turned cold, the moon hidden behind heavy cloud cover, frost shining on brown autumnal grass.

McLure had said good night to Fargo, thanked him for his help and set off for the main house. Fargo walked downriver to where he'd tied his stallion.

He was within five yards of his horse when he heard something snap in the wooded area to his left.

Instinctively, he pivoted toward the sound, grabbing his Colt as he did so. His sky blue eyes narrowed to better penetrate the wall of darkness. There was something—or somebody—in there.

Fargo raised his Colt, aiming at the exact center of the span of trees and brush that confronted him.

"You better come out of there, mister. Or I'll start firing."

This was all a bluff. Fargo had no idea where the

man—of course it might be a rabbit or a dog—might be in there. The puzzling thing was that the creature, whatever it might be, had made no other move since.

"Please don't shoot."

A soft, sweet voice. A woman, and a young one. His first thought was: *Trap*. He'd use the woman to calm Fargo down a bit, and when she stepped out, her male partner would, too, and shoot at Fargo.

"Get out here."

"I just want to talk to you."

"I'll only talk when I can see you."

"I'm afraid. Maybe this was a bad idea."

"I'll be the judge of that. Just get out here."

She wasn't deep behind the trees. Her soft voice was too clear for that. So it didn't take her long to work her way out of the brush and step down to the shoreline.

Fargo put her age at about twenty-two, twenty-three. She was a dark-haired woman with a fetching body covered in a buckskin jacket, a work shirt, butternuts and Western boots. Her blue eyes were as soft as her voice, as soft as her inviting lips.

"Who are you?" Fargo said.

"Beth Farrell. I'm one of the maids at the house up there. David would kill me if he knew I was down here talking to you."

"You dress like this all the time?"

"Oh, no. I usually wear my maid's uniform during the day and at night I stay in my room in the attic and read. I just wear my nightgown then." She smiled for the first time. The smile was as lush as the blue gaze. The clouds had fled past the moon so he now had a good look at her.

"You sneak out to see what was going on?"

She nodded. "Everybody did. As soon as we heard that somebody had killed Miss Bonnie."

Her tone was hard to read. She'd kept it neutral so that he couldn't tell what her opinion of Bonnie was.

"You knew her well?"

"Well, I worked with her every day."

"Did you like her?"

"She was a McLure. That's about all you can say for any of them. They forget that they come from the land

55

just like all of us do. But they got lucky because old man McLure was smart in terms of business."

"You hate her enough to kill her?"

She laughed. "Oh, good Lord, did I give that impression? That I hated her? I didn't. If I hated anybody, it was David's wife. She was nice to me at the beginning but then things changed. She's going to fire me soon. She's been talking to other women who do maid work."

She shivered. "I wish I was up in my attic room now."

"You could've gone to your room a long time ago. Why did you wait out here in the cold?"

"Because—" She hesitated. Just then a large animal— Fargo guessed a wild dog—tramped through the woods right behind the Farrell woman, startling and scaring her. She jumped forward a few feet, stumbling as she did so, right into Fargo's arms.

"You all right?"

"Yes." She was breathless now. "Lord, this whole night is so spooky. I guess Miss Bonnie's murder and all—"

She was still in his arms. When she realized this, she stood back from him, looking prim as she did so. "I'm sorry I tripped into you that way, Mr. Fargo."

He grinned. "I'm not."

She must have been feeling the same heat he did because after he holstered his gun and held his arms out to her, she came to him eagerly. "It's pretty cold for this."

"I'll bet we can figure out a way to warm up."

She smiled. "I guess I should sneak out of the attic more often. I haven't been with a man for a long time. C'mon, there's a small gazebo in the back of the mansion."

Fargo liked to vary his sexual encounters. Change women, change locales. He couldn't ever remember sexing a woman in a gazebo before. Another fine memory for his old age—if somebody didn't gun him down first.

She even took his hand as she led him up the slight incline that led to the east side of the mansion that stood against the night sky like a castle ready to repel all those who meant its inhabitants harm.

It had been a long time since he'd simply held hands

with a woman. He enjoyed it to the degree that he could already feel himself pushing against the constraints of his pants. The tension finally culminated in him simply grabbing her and kissing her with enough fervor to feel her give in and slip to the ground. They'd never make it to the gazebo and right now neither of them gave a damn.

They lay side by side, Fargo with his leg between hers with enough force that he could feel the heat and moisture between her legs. She hadn't been kidding. She hadn't been with a man for a while.

As they continued to kiss, his hands began unbuttoning her blouse. She wore no undergarments. His hands were filled with the bounty of her silken breasts. This pleased her to the point that she grabbed the wrist of his left hand and moved it down to the buttons of her butternuts.

He began undoing the buttons at once, his fingers trembling eagerly as they sought the treasure of her womanhood. It was softer, wetter and tighter than he could have wished for. She immediately began bucking against the finger he worked on her. Her gasping pushed the warm gentle air of her mouth over the side of his face. By this time they'd both forgotten about the cold weather.

Not even the frost against their buttocks, as they rolled over and over and Fargo disabused himself of his pants, bothered them. There was no other reality now than the shaft his manhood was creating inside her, deeper and deeper, wetter and wetter. She had to restrain herself from crying out on the late-night air. David McLure would come racing out of the house for sure, probably with a shotgun.

He wanted to hold off exploding—though that took some doing—so he could get even deeper inside her. He turned her on her side, moved one leg straight out and found the one true way to get maximum depth. As he began ramming harder and harder, he also took the time to begin kneading her buttocks, squeezing them with great strength. This translated into her making sexual noises he couldn't ever remember hearing before—the animal levels that all lovers hope to reach with each other. It was the most wonderful feeling of insanity—blind, gasping, pounding insanity—in the world.

She reached behind herself now and grabbed his shaft the first time she had a chance. She squeezed, indicating that she hoped he could hold off for a while longer. Then she began slowly pulling away from him, the back-door approach to lovemaking leaving him kneeling there with his shaft sticking straight out.

She knew what she wanted to do and she wasted no time doing it. She turned around and crawled back to him, facing him now, and then bowed her head and went to work on him with an oral magic he'd almost forgotten was possible.

He nearly fell over backward when her lips enveloped his manhood. Either she affected the mask of a virginal young prairie girl or she'd had a lot more men than she'd let on. The flick of her tongue, the grasp of his spear, the touch of the manhood that dangled down inside its sac—he was entering that realm of blind insanity again.

She took him as deep as his spear had thrust into her. And she, too, used buttocks as a way of enhancing the thrills her mouth blessed him with—grabbing his buttocks and squeezing almost painfully.

And when he could hold back no more, she gently put one hand on his chest and pushed him backward, so that he landed on his back while his senses began clashing—he lived in the most encapsulated moment any human being can experience—he was nothing but a vessel of pleasure because she hadn't given up yet, swallowing all he'd given her, but continuing to use her mouth and hands to sustain the thrill as he lay on the ground.

Exhausted, sweating even in the chill night, she lay next to him on the frosty grass.

Fargo lighted a cigarette he'd smoked half of previously. No sense rolling a new one when this one still had a lot of smoking left to yield.

"I'll remember this for a long time," she said, "if I can ever catch my breath again."

"You're a very special lady."

"Thank you. And you're a very special man. You'll be leaving town soon, I suppose."

"That's sort of been the pattern most of my life. I guess I just have to see what's over the next hill."

"And you ride alone."

"So far I do, anyway."

"I want my own home and children."

"No husband?"

She laughed. "The men I've seen around here are a pretty sorry lot."

"You mind if I ask you a question?"

"I knew we'd get around to that sooner or later."

"You did?"

"Sure. You want to know what I think about Mr. McLure getting killed and now Bonnie. But I'm getting chilly. Real chilly. Why don't we pull up our pants and button up better?"

"Talked me into it. I was noticing the cold myself."

Within two minutes, they were into their clothes and standing up again. They both slipped their gloves on. Beth stepped behind a tree that protected her from the wind that had just come up. Fargo followed her. He knew he had to ask his questions now—questions he'd been wanting to ask since he'd first seen her—he just hoped she'd cooperate.

"Why don't you tell me what you think about these murders now? You're in a good position to know more than just about anybody, seeing's how they both happened on the estate out here."

Her brow furrowed. "I know more than I should—more than I want to. But I don't know how much I should tell you. I'm afraid!"

"Beth! Beth! Where are you?"

"Oh, Lord, that's David McLure. I don't want him to see us together. He'll think I was telling you things."

"Beth!" McLure called again.

"Over here, David!" She turned to Fargo. "You need to go. Right away. Just run down to the dock. I'll stall him here."

"Can you see me after he goes?"

"No, Skye. I'll have to walk back to the house with him."

"What the hell are you doing out here?" David snapped before he even came into view.

Fargo knew he had no choice but to leave. He wasn't happy about that at all. He sensed she knew some vital secrets and he meant for her to share them.

But she was right. It would be awkward to be found here with him—awkward for her. And he didn't want to get her in any trouble.

He nodded to her and started moving fast to the downslope and the shoreline. The trouble was the frosty grass. Easy to slip on it and break something. He ran as fast as caution allowed.

"I asked what the hell are you doing out here," David spat. "You get back to the house right now. And I expect a good explanation."

Fargo's stomach churned. McLure talked to her like she was a bad child—or a slave. Nobody deserved that kind of treatment, especially not from a man born into money and influence—a man who'd done nothing of his own to earn it.

But Fargo knew he was finished with her. He rode back to town, his jaw muscles still grinding over David McLure's treatment of Beth Farrell.

David McLure's wife, Sarah, already in place inside the huge canopy bed, was reading a book and trying to summon sufficient solemnity for the moment. It wasn't easy. Bonnie had always resented her. Bonnie had imagined, apparently, that there would always be only the three of them—Dad, David and herself. She was one of those women who resented the presence of other women. From things David had said, Bonnie hadn't been all that unhappy when her mother died. One less female around the house.

David went about slamming doors, sighing and cursing under his breath. Sarah kept trying to come up with appropriate facial expressions—the wake and the funeral would try her best acting skills.

Too late, she realized that David was offended by what she was doing, no matter what expression she chose to wear.

"My sister's been murdered and you lie there reading one of your stupid romances."

"Oh, David, please. Don't make things worse by going into one of your snits."

"A man is grieving for his sister and you call it a 'snit.'"

"Yes, this is a snit. You're looking for somebody to take your grief out on, and since I'm the only one handy, you're putting it on me." She decided to be marginally honest. She laid her book, open, on her lap. In her white sleeping gown, her hair brushed long for the night, she looked quite fetching. "I'm not going to pretend that Bonnie and I were the best of friends. We weren't. If you're honest about it, I tried to be her friend when I first came here but she wouldn't have it. But I'm very sorry that she's dead because I know what this is going to do to you—already has done to you. I've never seen you look like this. It makes me sad for you, honey, and it scares me, too. You're a sensible man. At least under most circumstances. But tonight when you came up here and told me that they'd found her dead—"

David sank to a chair. He put his elbows on his knees and his face into his hands.

"Did you find anything in the boathouse when you went back through it?"

Her words had calmed him. He sighed and took his face from his hands. "Yes. I learned that Harvey is even more of a fool than I'd thought. There was a man named Fargo with us—the one who was supposed to meet Bonnie. He knows a lot more about investigations than Harvey does."

"Can he help you?"

"I was thinking about that, actually."

He lay back in the chair, stretched out his long legs, stared at the ceiling. "I just think of all the nasty things I said to her over the years."

"Try and remember some of the nasty things she said to you. She didn't exactly cut you much slack."

"That doesn't help right now. I can be a prig sometimes."

Yes, you can, Sarah thought, but she said, "That's ridiculous. If you mean that you feel guilty about trying to get her to live a respectable life—you were doing what any older brother would. I don't want you to punish yourself about this. She was a troubled girl with a troubled history. You were more than understanding. As was your father. A lot of families would have just put her out on the street."

He sat up straight in the chair and said, "I guess I'll go down to the library and have a drink."

"You probably need one."

He smiled. "Thanks for putting up with me. I know I can be a pain sometimes."

"You could always come over here and kiss me."

"Now that doesn't sound like a bad idea at all."

"Maybe you could get that drink a little later." When she held her arms out to him, he saw the shape of her wonderful breasts and the faint pink color of her nipples through the sheer fabric of her sleeping gown.

He decided that this was a much better idea than having a drink.

A much better idea.

"Oh, God, Theo, I hope you're not involved in this in any way."

These were Helen's first words to Mason tonight and they shamed him. He had humiliated her so many times with his affairs and still she stood by him. Now she was worried that he would somehow be implicated in Bonnie's murder.

She helped Mason off with his coat and hung it up for him. "Would you like some coffee?"

"That sounds good." Then he reached out and took her by her wrists and drew her to him. "You deserve a lot better husband than me."

She slipped from his grasp. "Tell me everything that happened tonight over coffee. I think there's some pound cake left, too."

It had been a long time since Theo Mason had appreciated his home, the beauty of its decoration, the high style of its furnishings, the gentle atmosphere that Helen created by her very presence. He promised himself, as he'd promised himself so many times before, that he really would become a better husband.

The living room complemented the Queen Anne style of the exterior. He loved this room with its matching overstuffed sofas and the soft light of the lamps and the somber tones of the grandfather clock. Even the cuckoo clock, which he'd hated at first, had come to comfort him on nights when the pressures of the day seemed to offer no other solace.

He owed everything to Helen. He'd become wealthy because of her father. At the outset he had seen himself as a very cunning young fellow, but as the marriage had progressed, he saw that he was little more than a serf to her powerful father, Jayce Cunningham. But through it all—bad and good alike—Helen stood by him.

He walked to the small bar in the corner by the enormous fireplace. Here the smoky scent was almost a narcotic. You could close your eyes and be carried away with it, the way Chinese men in the big cities claimed to be carried away to another dimension with opium.

Tonight he let himself be carried away with a triple shot of bourbon poured into a clean glass.

He walked over to the largest of the sofas and sat down. Helen brought in a serving tray with coffee and pound cake and said, "I'm sorry she's dead, Theo. Even though she tried to take you away from me, she didn't deserve this."

She poured coffee and cut each of them a thin slice of cake, then seated herself next to him on the long sofa and said, "What happened tonight?"

That was when it all began to suffocate Mason, everything that had happened in these past few days. He looked at his wife, realizing again what a fine, fine woman she was, and said, tears starting to stream down his cheeks, "I've made a mess of our marriage, haven't I?"

She laid her soft hand on the right side of his face and said, "We still love each other, Theo. That's all that matters."

But there was something in her voice . . . something she wasn't saying. And then he realized what had happened. "You already knew most of the things I told you, didn't you?"

"I wanted to hear you tell me. Father was here earlier."

"Oh, God. He probably thinks I did it, doesn't he?"

She took his hands in hers. "You know how he reacts to things. He blusters for an hour and then calms down. And he didn't accuse you of murdering Bonnie—he just said . . ."

"Said what?" He could barely speak. Her father held Theo's future in his hands. He could crush Theo any time he wanted.

She averted her eyes when she spoke. "He just said that this was what you get for spending time with other women—and what I get for not leaving you."

And then she said the worst thing of all: "I'm pretty sure you'll be seeing him sooner than later."

10

Fargo had just finished shaving when somebody knocked on his hotel room door. He dipped his razor into the washbasin, splashed off the shaving soap, then toweled off his face. He grabbed his shirt and went to the door.

He had no idea who the woman was, but she certainly had an air of quiet importance, the kind of quiet importance that only money can inspire. She was pleasantly pretty, though no beauty, dressed in a frilly white blouse and dark blue skirt. A dark blue shawl was draped over her shoulders.

"Are you Mr. Fargo?"

"Yes, ma'am."

"My name is Helen Mason." She hesitated a moment. "My husband is Theo Mason."

Stranger and stranger, Fargo thought. What the hell was she doing here?

"I need to talk to you but I'm not sure it's appropriate that we do it in your room. Would you meet me downstairs in the café in five minutes?"

"Ma'am, I'm not sure what this is all about."

For the first time, he saw the redness at the base of her eyes and the tear wrinkles of the flesh beneath. She'd been crying.

"You haven't heard about Theo?"

"No, ma'am, I guess not."

"He's been arrested for murdering Bonnie McLure and her father."

She turned then and walked away.

* * *

65

Fargo said, after ordering his coffee, eggs and sliced potatoes, "So when did this happen, Mrs. Mason?"

"Please, call me Helen."

Fargo nodded.

"The middle of the night," she went on. "We were in bed asleep. And they started pounding on the door, and I do mean pounding. They sounded as if they were trying to break the door down. Naturally, we were both terrified. We didn't have any idea of who they were or what they planned to do with us. We both put on robes and went downstairs. My husband brought his shotgun along. The first thing we did was go to the window in the living room and peek out. It looked like the Klan. There were three or four of them with torches and two or three more with shotguns. Harvey was the one at the door doing the pounding.

"Theo got mad. He's always supported Harvey—I always thought Harvey was a fool and now I feel that more than ever—and he just couldn't believe that Harvey would try something like this. He opened the door and Harvey charged in. One of his deputies was right behind him and he grabbed my husband's shotgun and then shoved him against the wall. In our own home. It was like a nightmare. None of it made any sense. Harvey said that they'd found the gun used to kill both Mr. McLure and Bonnie. It's a special Colt that belonged to Theo's father, who was a colonel for the Confederacy.

"And then Harvey got all sanctimonious the way he does and said that he was arresting Theo for the murders of Bonnie McLure and Mr. McLure. The doc took the bullets out of both of them and they matched the only kind of bullets Theo can use in his father's gun. I think we both said, 'That's ridiculous,' at the same time. But Harvey was serious. He had one of his other deputies handcuff Theo and then he sort of apologized to me.

"Theo didn't handle it as well as he could have, I suppose. Rather than trying to keep Harvey on an even keel, he started insulting him. Telling him what a joke he was to most people in the town and how he was going to have Harvey fired first thing in the morning. And then—oh, God, I hate even thinking about this—he spit on Harvey. Right in the face. And right in front of two of the deputies.

"The funny thing is that Harvey managed to control himself. He just took out his handkerchief and wiped off the spittle and said—and he was so calm it was scarier than if he'd been angry—'We'll talk about this later, Theo.' I didn't remember till later what that meant, how Harvey always takes prisoners into that little room he has and beats them half to death. I know that he once beat a man so badly, he blinded the man permanently."

"Then he took him away?"

"Yes."

"Have you seen your husband since?"

"I tried. Harvey wasn't there but the deputy on duty said that Harvey had left instructions that nobody was to see Theo under any circumstances. I'm sure he had me in mind when he said it. And that's when I came to you."

"How did you even know about me?"

"As Harvey was dragging him away—Theo put up quite a fight—Theo said under his breath, 'Tell Fargo I need help.' It didn't make any sense to me at the time but now it does."

"Well, then you know a lot more than I do."

The waiter came with the food.

"You sure you don't want anything, Helen?"

"Just this coffee, Mr. Fargo."

"Skye."

Quick, nervous smile. "Skye."

Fargo chowed down. He was hungry. He tried not to smack his lips. A man who eats alone most of the time develops some real antisocial habits.

"Why he asked for you is because the people who run this town have turned against him. And I know why."

He kept his fork two inches from his mouth. A delicious bite of egg and potato awaited him. "Why?"

"My father."

"Your father?"

She then explained that her father was as wealthy and powerful as the McLure clan. And he'd never liked Theo.

"My father's friends are going to make it very tough for Theo."

"Theo's a smart man and he'll get a good lawyer."

"Not if he doesn't have the money, he won't."

"He doesn't have money?"

"He has the bank's money. Very little of his own. Father has kept us going with what he calls 'gifts' from time to time. He gives them to us because of me, not because of Theo. Despite Theo. Theo isn't very good at handling money."

Fargo couldn't help himself. He laughed. "A bank president who isn't very good at handling money?"

"My father got him that job. He thought that I deserved a husband who was an important man in the community. He uses that phrase a lot: 'an important man in the community.' Those are the only people he'll associate with. He forgets that he came from nothing. He forgets on purpose. He doesn't want to remember when he was just another poor boy struggling to make his way in the world. He's convinced himself somehow that he came from an important family and that he's always been rich."

"And you really think he'll go through with this—he won't back down?"

"You don't know my father, Skye. He's the most vindictive man I know. And he wants to pay Theo back for cheating on me all these years."

Fargo sat back in his chair, took the makings out and rolled himself a cigarette. "I'm still not sure what I can do for your husband."

"He was telling me last night how you showed Harvey up by talking about Scotland Yard and how they handle a murder investigation."

"I was just quoting what I'd read. That doesn't make me an operative."

"That makes you more of an operative than old Harvey. He'll be glad that my father forced him to set Theo up for the murder. Now Harvey won't have to do any actual work, which he probably wouldn't have done, anyway."

He admired her composure. No tears, no hysterics.

"You could just ask around about things, Skye. Find out what Bonnie did in the last few hours of her life. I'm sure if we knew that, we'd know who the killer was."

Fargo took a deep drag of his smoke. "I had the same thought myself. Somebody either knew that she was going to meet me at the boathouse or somebody had been watching her house and saw her leave. And followed her to the boathouse. And killed her."

"You sound interested."

"I am interested. To be honest, I don't care much for your husband but I hate to see him blamed for something he didn't do. And I'm just plain curious about Bonnie's death. She wasn't easy to get along with. She must've made a lot of enemies. I'm just wondering which one of them killed her."

"She had an enemy right in the house there. David McLure's wife couldn't stand her."

"What would her motive be?"

"I think she just wants to move. She didn't like his father at all. She comes from a very refined family. Old man McLure was pretty vulgar. And domineering. Bonnie always took her father's part. She hated Sarah." She started to say something, then stopped herself. "I just thought of something."

"What?"

"With old man McLure dead and Bonnie murdered, maybe Sarah won't care about moving now. She'll be running the household. She won't have to put up with the McLures dictating everything."

She reached into the small leather purse she'd been carrying, took out an envelope and slid it across the table to Fargo. "Two hundred fifty down and five hundred more if you help me find out who really killed Bonnie. Thank God I always set something aside that I don't tell Theo about."

"What if I can't find the killer?"

"Then I've wasted two hundred and fifty dollars and you've wasted your time. But I have more faith in you than that."

Fargo didn't want to be coy. He knew he was going to help her and he knew that the two hundred and fifty would treat him real nice. He didn't need a fortune to improve his lifestyle. He said, "I still think I'm taking this under false pretenses. I'm not an operative."

"No, but as I said, Skye, you're more of an operative than anybody else in this town is. And that gives us more of a chance of finding the killer, especially if we start right away before the trail gets cold."

He looked at the envelope lying there. It represented a lot of hotel rooms with decent beds and a lot of restaurant steak dinners and more than a few nights drinking the time away with the ladies of his choice.

"I'll do my best, Helen."

"That's all I can ask, Skye."

11

Theo Mason had always lived with the secret fear that someday he would be discovered as an imposter—not as smart, not as clever as he was generally perceived—and that his life, exposed for all to see, would come to a terrible end.

Well, he thought as he lay on his bunk in the jailhouse, it had finally happened.

He'd been arrested for murder.

"You know who I think that is?"

There were two of them in the next cell and they were the scum of the earth. Filthy, ragged losers with no teeth, open sores on their necks and hands, hair that was a rat's nest of grime. He could smell them from his cell.

"I think that there's that there banker."

"A banker? They wouldn't put no banker in jail."

So far, they'd been speaking in whispers. Not that Mason couldn't hear every word.

But now they were speaking in regular voices.

"Hey," one said, "you that there banker fella?"

"He shore is."

"Hey, mister, you hear me? Are you that there banker fella?"

Mason kept his eyes closed. "You want a loan? Is that it?"

They giggled like children.

"See, I told ya it was him."

"How come they put a banker in jail?"

"I was arrested for killing two really irritating pieces of human scum like you two."

There was a pause.

"Hey, did you just insult us?"

"Sure sounded that way to me," Mason said. This was a distraction and he was thankful for it. Better than lying here and thinking of a trial—and of being hanged.

"See, he even admits it."

"Well, mister, you just better hope me and Earle here never catch you when we get out of here."

"We don't take to nobody who calls us 'scum.' "

"Yeah, our family's got some pride."

But the distraction was fading. Now it was just listening to the raspy voices of two probably murderous hayseeds, though they were in here, from what he could tell, on charges of drunk and disorderly.

"How about you boys shut up for a while?"

"It's a free country. We can talk all we want."

"Yeah, just like Earle said, it's a free country."

And then one of them farted with the force of a cannonball being fired.

They were giggling again. One of them—and it didn't matter which one—said, "It's a free country is right and I can fart all I want."

Mason realized he was in hell. Stupid scumbags like these were the type of people he'd meet in prison. Even if he didn't hang, these were the sort of men he'd spend the rest of his life with.

He didn't hear the deputy until the deputy had slid the key in the cell door lock and turned it.

"C'mon, Mr. Mason, Marshal said to bring you up to his office."

Mason wondered if this would be the moment he dreaded most of all. Being alone with Harvey. And Harvey beating a confession out of him. Mason had no doubt that he would confess to anything after being worked over by Harvey. Nobody could withstand that kind of punishment. Especially not a man as weak as Mason, a man who was accustomed to using his power— not his fists—to get what he wanted.

"If you smell anything, Deppity, it's 'cause my brother Earle just farted."

The scumbags giggled.

"You having a good time with these two gents, Mr. Mason?" the deputy said. Obviously, he was treating

Mason much better than he'd treat the average prisoner.
And with good reason. What if the town marshal was
wrong and Mr. Mason was not only found innocent but
returned to the bank with all that power?

You think Mr. Mason wouldn't remember a deputy
who'd treated him badly?

"You go right on up, Mr. Mason," the deputy said.
"I'll be right up."

"Sure smells in here," one of the brothers giggled.

Mason started walking toward the front of the place.
Over his shoulder, he said, "Why does Harvey want to
see me?"

"Oh, it ain't the marshal, Mr. Mason. It's your father-
in-law."

Mason felt stunned by the words.

His father-in-law?

What was going on here?

Dread filled him. And then fear. And he couldn't have
told you why exactly. He just knew that this was going
to be very, very bad.

Fargo ground-tied his stallion a hundred yards down
the beach from the boathouse. The autumn day was bril-
liant with lemon-colored sunlight and perfect blue sky.
All along the shore the trees were colorful with the first
fire of the new season. The river was mostly blue, too.
There weren't many factories in this area dumping their
waste into the nearest body of water.

Fargo walked along in the sand toward the boathouse.
He wished this was a happier occasion so he could enjoy
himself. But he took his tasks seriously. Even though he
didn't care much for Theo Mason, he felt that the man
probably was being framed by person or persons un-
known. And he was being well paid to find out who had
done the framing.

In the daylight, the wooden structure showed its age
in various ways—the toll the water had taken on the
lower parts of the boathouse, some of the wood split
open and covered with moss; the roof in need of new
shingles; one of the windows patched with tape.

He climbed aboard the boathouse and instantly, in
response to a sound from within, drew his gun.

He listened as somebody inside moved around.

He eased over to the door, put his hand on the knob and then flung it backward.

She was not only beautiful; she was tough enough not to be intimidated by a man with a gun. "You look like somebody on a dime novel cover. But as fierce as you look, I have to say I don't have any money. It's up at the house." She smiled.

Fargo slipped his gun back into his holster. "Sorry. You just never know what you'll find on the other side of a door."

"I'm almost disappointed that you're not going to shoot me. And by the way, should I know who you are?"

"My name's Fargo, ma'am."

"Oh, the mysterious Mr. Fargo. People talk about you all the time. Harvey's got everybody convinced you're a complete menace to our little society here. He says you're a very bad man."

"Good old Harvey."

She was so damned pretty and regal it was difficult to pay any attention to her words. She was the Eastern magazine lady you saw in all the spreads about life in the upper classes, the chestnut-colored hair pulled back in a prim bun, the elegant face complemented by the almost severe simplicity of the blue suede jacket, the white blouse beneath and the gray butternuts that fed into calf-length riding boots.

"I take it you don't care for Harvey, Mr. Fargo?"

"You don't sound as if you do, either."

"He's our protector from the riffraff, as my dear departed father-in-law always said. He always seemed to forget that he'd been riffraff for a good part of his life."

"That happens to rich people sometimes."

"My"—and she sounded amused—"you sound like a socialist."

"I'd just like to see everybody get a fair shake is all. I see a lot of hungry people in my travels."

"You seem very noble, Mr. Fargo. And now, as lady of the house, I need to ask what you're doing here on my property."

"Just seeing if anything got overlooked."

"That doesn't answer my question, Mr. Fargo. I want to know what your interest is in this."

"I'm helping Helen Mason."

She ruined her beauty by frowning. "I'm afraid I don't have much respect for Helen. Nor do most of the women in this town."

"You mean the women who count?"

"Even though you're being sarcastic, that's exactly what I mean. None of the women I know would ever put up with how Theo has embarrassed her over the years. Bonnie was the same way. She saw whom she pleased and propriety be damned. She didn't even care what her father thought."

"How about your husband? Did she care what he thought?"

"My husband loved his sister. But that didn't mean that he approved of how she lived her life."

"And now he inherits the entire estate?"

She offered him an icy smile. "I see the gossips are at work already. I suppose that gives them something to do with their dreary lives. But since there hasn't been a reading of Bonnie's will yet, we don't know any more than the gossips do."

He scanned the boathouse. Nothing seemed out of place. A stack of three rowboats on either side of the place. A couple of yellow rain slickers with matching caps hanging on hooks. A pile of oars in one corner. A rowboat turned upside down and set on wooden saw-horses. A hole in the bottom was being patched.

He was about to ask her more questions about Bonnie when he heard somebody walk on the dock and head toward the boathouse.

Neither of them said anything. The door opened and a man stuck his head inside. Fargo recognized him from last night—David McLure.

"Well," he said, "this is a surprise. My wife in the boathouse with another man." He tried to make it sound like a joke. But all three of them knew it was no joke at all. He looked at Fargo now. "I guess I won't be needing your help after all, Mr. Fargo, because Harvey proved to my satisfaction that Theo killed my sister. I also learned that you're helping Helen Mason."

"That's my business who I help," Fargo said.

Today McLure wore range clothes—a blue flannel shirt, jeans, boots and a low-brimmed hat. His hand rested on the handle of the six-gun that sat in his holster.

"I guess I shouldn't have expected you to understand honor, Mr. Fargo. That was stupid of me." He took his wife's arm. "Why don't you go spend some of that money Helen gave you? She's a generous woman. A foolish woman—but generous."

"Good day, Mr. Fargo," the wife said. "Let's go for a walk along the shore, dear. I'm sure Mr. Fargo can find his way off our property."

Which is just what Fargo did.

Fargo was about twenty yards from the isolated cabin that sat along the river when somebody opened fire with a repeater.

The bullets weren't meant to kill, only to warn, but they came close enough that an accident could wound or even kill him.

He grabbed his Henry, dropped from his stallion and ran to a pair of oaks for protection.

He decided the best thing he could do was put on a demonstration of some really fancy shooting. He shot out both cabin windows. He bent the tin chimney. He stampeded the three horses in the rope corral. And finally he demolished the lock on the front door.

He was surprised by what happened next. A slender man who couldn't be more than twenty or twenty-one came out of the cabin with his repeater dangling from one hand, the barrel pointed to the ground. He wore an expensive blue shirt that buttoned down the side, a pair of gray butternuts and a fancy pair of black boots, made just for him no doubt.

And he was damned mad. "What the hell you think you're doing?"

"What the hell do you think you're doing?"

"You could've killed me."

"If I'd wanted you dead, you'd be dead by now. Take my word for it, kid."

"Don't call me 'kid.' "

"Yes, sir, commander. Now drop that rifle and pitch your Colt into that buffalo grass over there."

"That's not fair."

He sounded like a damned five-year-old throwing a fit.

"What's not fair?"

"I ran out of bullets for my repeater. I bet you've still got plenty of bullets."

"Who ever told you life was fair, kid?"

"I warned you about 'kid.'"

"Yeah. I warned you about tossing your guns. Now do it."

As he watched Davis pitch his weapons, he wondered what the hell a rich boy was doing living in a shack like this. The grass was knee-high. The well had been toppled. And you could see water marks on the cabin itself from spring flooding. The cabin had been built way too close to the river behind it.

Glen Davis had been Bonnie McLure's fiancé. He'd been seen arguing bitterly with her shortly before she was murdered. He was definitely near the top of the suspect list.

When Davis was done with his weapons, Fargo came out from behind the trees. He kept his Colt leveled right at Davis' chest.

"You're supposed to have a lot of money, Davis. What're you doing out here?"

"Who the hell're you? You look like a saddle tramp."

"I wouldn't push the insults, kid. In case you haven't noticed, I've got a gun and you don't."

"Charlie at the saloon tell you where I was?"

"Doesn't matter who told me. I found you. That's what matters."

"It was Charlie. He wasn't supposed to tell anybody." He was handsome in a spoiled sort of way. He pouted like a woman, an attribute that wasn't about to win him admirers among men. "I came out here to show Bonnie that I wasn't as much of a spoiled brat as she said. I bet her a hundred dollars I could live out here by myself for a month and do just fine."

"Why'd you kill her?"

"You bastard. You know better than that."

"No, I don't. You slapped her and her brother had to break it up."

"Her brother. What a sanctimonious bastard he is. And slapping a woman is a long ways from killing her."

"Sometimes it is. But not always. Maybe you followed her to the boathouse and killed her."

"From what I hear they've already arrested Theo Mason. And he's a lot more logical for the killer than I am. She's been sleeping with him on and off for a couple of years. He was the reason we fought so much. She wouldn't let go of him."

Fargo thought about what Davis had just said. "How'd you hear about Mason out here?"

Davis ran a shaky hand through his sun-streaked blond hair. "Just say I have my ways of getting information." For the first time, he sounded nervous.

Fargo laughed. "There're a number of ranches around here. Is that how you get your grub? You pay them and they feed you?"

"That's not any of your business." But the blush on his cheeks told Fargo that his guess had been good.

"And I bet you sleep in the bunkhouse, don't you?"

"I said that that was none of your business."

"Yeah, you're roughing it, all right. I'll bet you don't spend more than a few hours a day out here. Life's a lot better on a ranch, isn't it?"

The pout again. "Well, it was a stupid bet to begin with. So what if I don't actually live out here? There's nothing to do and there're so many animals roaming around at night, I'd never get to sleep. I'm moving back home tonight."

Fargo laughed. "You're some piece of work, kid."

This time Davis didn't object to "kid."

Fargo said, "Where were you last night?"

"Over at the Bar D."

"You can prove it?"

"You ask a man named Shorty. He'll tell you."

"I'll make a point of asking him. The other thing is that you don't seem all that broken up about Bonnie."

"You wouldn't be broken up, either, if some little tramp told you that she'd been sleeping with Mason again."

"Pretty good motive for killing her, wouldn't you say?"

"They've got Mason. Harvey won't come after me. And anyway, Shorty'll swear to where I was."

"How much did you pay him?"

The blush again. But he didn't say anything.

Fargo said, "This isn't over, kid. Harvey may have Mason in jail but that doesn't mean Mason is the killer."

"Harvey wouldn't arrest anybody as important as Theo unless he thought he really had a case against him. He's almost never wrong."

" 'Almost,' huh? That means he's wrong sometimes. And he's wrong in this case."

"You working for Mason?"

"Yeah."

The kid smirked. "So you wouldn't be a little bit prejudiced on his side?"

"Sure I am. But from what I've been able to find out so far, Harvey arrested him with no real evidence. I'm thinking somebody put Harvey up to it. And I'm going to find out who."

He started to turn away, then stopped. "I'm told your father is a very important man. Maybe he figured out that you killed Bonnie and he bribed Harvey to arrest Theo. You think that's a possibility?"

"Get the hell out of here. I'm sick of you."

"My name's Fargo, kid. And you're gonna be a lot more sick of me by the time this is all over."

This time when he turned away, Fargo walked back to the oak where he'd left his Henry. A few minutes later, he was on his stallion and headed back to town.

Helen Mason said, "I want to see my husband, Harvey."

"I'm afraid I can't let you do that, Helen. Not until I'm done talking to him a few more times."

"If you've been beating him, Harvey, I swear to God I'll kill you."

Harvey DeLong smiled. "You're a cultured woman, Helen. I wouldn't expect you to talk that way."

"There's a man named Fargo."

"Oh, yes, Mr. Fargo."

"He's been a big help to me. More than you have."

Harvey sighed and put on his civil service face. "I know this is hard for you, Helen. And I'm sorry for it. Just seeing you standing here in my office makes me feel bad for you. You don't belong in a marshal's office. Not a refined woman like you. But I'm just doing my job. I have evidence that your husband murdered Bonnie McLure. You're not going to deny that they'd been seeing each other, are you?"

She was silent for a time and then she said, "I didn't say what I wanted to about Skye Fargo. I've hired him to help me clear my husband's name. If you try to run him off again, I'll go straight to the men's club and tell them that I want and need him here to help me. And they won't refuse me, Harvey, because I'm one of them. The so-called carriage trade. They'll feel sorry for me and one of them will come over here and tell you to leave Fargo alone. So save everybody trouble, Harvey, and let Fargo do his job for me."

Harvey knew that what she said was true. The men's club, to which he'd never been invited, would to a man do anything they could to help Helen now. Pity, loyalty, whatever you wanted to call it—she was right when she said she was one of them by virtue of being married to Theo.

"What's your answer, Harvey?"

"Well," he said, a mean grin parting his lips, "you can't fight city hall. Or the men's club, I guess. Tell Fargo I won't bother him."

12

On the street, still a winsome fall day, Fargo stopped at a café for coffee and a piece of apple pie. He was just finishing up and rolling himself an after-eating cigarette when he saw one of the fanciest surreys he'd ever seen. For one thing, it was half again as big as most surreys and it was trimmed in what appeared to be gold. There was a seat in back facing out where a man with a shotgun sat. The driver was a huge and angry-looking man with a gray-shot black beard straight out of the Bible. The surrey was pulled by two enormous black draft horses.

Fargo said to the woman behind the café counter, "Looks like you folks have an emperor, huh?"

She laughed. "I can see where you'd think that. But that's how Jayce Cunningham operates. Larger than life. Everything about him. He goes to the county fair and he wins the rifle-shooting contest, the strength contest, the roping contest and the square dance contest—and he's well into his sixties."

So that had been his first glimpse of Helen's father. He saw now why old man McLure was considered so quiet and modest. Anybody would be quiet and modest compared to what he'd just seen.

"You think he's the most powerful man around here now that McLure is dead?"

"Hard to say. But he's close if he's not."

"Who'd be his competition?"

She had to think about it. "Cap Frazier, probably. He owns two short-haul railroads and makes a fortune every year. He'd probably be close. Or maybe he's even more powerful than Jayce. But I'd sure hate to tell that to Jayce."

"He kind of a hothead?"

She laughed again. "Are you kidding? You've never seen anybody mad until you've seen Jayce go off. People walk very, very softly around him. Like they're on eggshells. You never know what's going to make him mad so you've got to be real, real careful."

"Well, that's good to know."

"You have a special interest in Jayce?" For the first time, she sounded suspicious.

He smiled. "Nope. I've just never seen a surrey like that. I figured it had to be some kind of royalty."

"That's a good one. And come to think of it, that'd fit old Jayce real nice—being royalty like that."

Fargo paid his bill, thanked her and left.

Fargo knew he was being followed. The deputy had been waiting for him outside the café.

Fargo couldn't figure out if the man was just inept or if he really wanted Fargo to see him. Either way, Fargo wouldn't have hired him as a tail.

The Trailsman planned to ask some questions around Theo Mason's bank. See what the employee assessment was of Mason. He didn't want the deputy hanging around him. He decided to lose the man.

He walked the three blocks of the commercial part of town, then turned in an alley. He needed a quick-fast hiding place. He assumed he'd find a loading dock of some kind, but no luck. He had to settle for a wagon bed.

The deputy, gun drawn, entered the alley, looking warily about. He might be dumb but he wasn't dumb enough not to spot a trap. When somebody led you into an alley he was usually ready to shoot you. He had to be damned careful. This wasn't any saddle tramp he was following. This was the Trailsman. And the deputy had heard enough stories about the man to know that Fargo was dangerous as hell.

But Fargo had no intention of shooting anybody. He lay in the wagon bed, covered with a tarpaulin he'd found stuffed in a corner of the bed.

The deputy looked almost comic as he walked down

the alley, jerking and jumping at the slightest sound, pivoting and crouching to fire at enemies that weren't there. Once, he tripped over his own feet. This time when he searched the alley with his nervous eyes he wasn't looking for enemies. He was looking to see if anybody had seen him trip.

Fargo had to give the deputy one thing. He was dogged. He must have walked up and down that alley six or seven times. A couple of times, Fargo sensed that the man had even peered into the wagon where Fargo was hiding. But apparently he wasn't curious enough to poke the tarpaulin he saw in there, something any good investigator would have done. Check every wagon thoroughly. But all the man did was snort and pass on.

Finally, the deputy seemed to be done. Seemed to be. Could he be smart enough to set a trap for Fargo? Pretend that he'd left the alley and then wait for Fargo to come out from his hiding place? Maybe.

Fargo had to be careful. He drew his Colt. He slowly eased out from under the tarpaulin, careful to keep his head down so it wouldn't show over the sides of the wagon.

He moved now by inches, crawling to the back of the wagon, making ready to roll off the back end without the deputy being able to spot him.

The ground was harder and dustier than Fargo had figured. He lay in the dirt for several minutes, waiting to see if the deputy had spotted him. But—nothing. No response.

Fargo slowly got to his feet, dusted himself off. And it was then that he saw the sun-glint. At first he wasn't sure what was sparkling in the sunlight. But soon enough he realized that it was a Colt much like his own. The deputy stood on the roof of a one-story warehouse halfway up the alley. He was looking away from Fargo's position. He hadn't seen Fargo escape the wagon.

Fargo was half tempted to give the man a shout. After all, this was a kind of game they were playing. Maybe the man would appreciate Fargo's sense of humor.

But then again, maybe not.

The best thing Fargo could do was get out of this alley and get to the bank.

There was no way the deputy could catch up with him now. Fargo very nonchalantly started walking out of his end of the alley. Not until he was about to disappear around the opening of the alley did the deputy spot him. Then he shouted, "Stop! Stop!"

Oh, yes, Fargo thought, this was exactly the man he'd hire to tail somebody. Tails didn't usually yell at the people they were trailing. Not in Fargo's world, they didn't.

13

The interior of Theo Mason's bank was attractive—mahogany wainscoting, handsome paintings of the mythic West, hardwood floors that shone like new pennies—but nothing was more attractive than the woman he asked for directions to the vice president's office.

She was one of those almost too-plush redheads who narrowly missed being buxom because of a small waist and surprisingly thin arms and wrists and hands and a narrow, fine neck. In a frilly blue blouse and a long tan skirt, she was every lonesome cowpoke's campfire dream, her lushness settling in all the right places, those being perfect breasts, the shapely bottom, and the beautifully freckled face with the somewhat coy brown eyes.

"I see that the vice president's name here is Cal Winthrop. I wonder if there's a chance I could talk to him."

"Is this about a loan or a deposit?"

"Afraid it's neither. I need to talk to him about Theo Mason."

"Oh."

He could tell that she'd kept her one-syllable response as neutral as possible.

"I see. Well, unfortunately—and I mean unfortunately for the bank—Mr. Winthrop has been at the county seat for the past two days and won't be back till tomorrow. I'm sure you know what happened to poor Mr. Mason. As soon as that misunderstanding is cleared up, he'll be back here himself."

"So you think it's a misunderstanding?"

"Of course. Mr. Mason didn't kill anybody. That's absurd. He's one of the most respected men in this part of the Territory. People like that don't murder people."

"Just lowlives kill people—is that what you're saying?"

She had been studying him with the same fervor he'd studied her. There was lively interest in the brown eyes.

An enormous smile revealed the sensuous shape of her large mouth. She said, "Yes, lowlives like you."

Fargo laughed. "You know who I am?"

"No. You've just got that look about you—dangerous. And why would I know who you are? Are you famous?"

"No. My name's Skye Fargo. Why I asked was I thought maybe Harvey DeLong had been by here to tell all you people not to answer any questions I asked you."

She shook her head. "If I had a nickel for every time that man patted my bottom—" She suddenly looked over his shoulder. "A very important customer just came in, Mr. Fargo. Tell you what. I'm free for lunch. I have forty-five minutes. Do you know where the Silver Dollar is?"

"I've walked past it a few times. Why don't you meet me there at eleven thirty?"

"Fine."

She touched one of her breasts in an almost shockingly erotic way. Her bosom seemed to swell with sudden excitement. "I like my men dangerous. That's why I always resisted Theo. He talks tough but he's basically a coward. And that's also why he's not a killer. He wouldn't have the nerve for it."

Then she was walking away, the wisps of her perfume as sensuous as the long fine fingers that had touched her breast.

Fargo was thinking that if they had forty-five minutes alone in his hotel room . . .

"Marshal, Jayce Cunningham is here to see you."

Harvey DeLong felt his bowels tighten. All his life he had served important men, men who played hell on your entire body when they wanted something from you—headaches, nausea, the trots, cold sweats. Sometimes it was a miserable life, being a whore for powerful men. But then you had to consider the money you made under the table, the association with power that in effect made you powerful—and the secrets. Ah, yes, the secrets. Even with the most important of men, when you knew their secrets they tended to be afraid of you. They'd never admit it but you could see that they were when you skillfully reminded them—just sneaking in a phrase or two—of what you had on them. They might tell you to shut up but it was easy to see that they feared you for sure.

Harvey pushed himself up from his chair and said, "Tell him to come back."

"He don't look in an especially good mood."

Harvey snorted. "He never looks to be in an especially good mood, does he?"

"Well, I didn't want to say it this way—but right now, he looks outright mad, Marshal. I just wanted to warn you."

"Bring him back. I'll do what I can for him."

"All right, Marshal."

Harvey could hear Jayce's thunderous voice complaining about something. He couldn't tell exactly what had pissed off the big bastard but the tone definitely carried the message that he was displeased with something. Harvey's bowels stirred again. He patted his stomach. Sometimes he just wanted to take a gun to every important man he'd ever served and—

Jayce walked with the gait of a giant, plodding, heavy-footed, each step conveying anger. The last might be something Harvey imagined but he could be excused for such a fantasy because everything else about Jayce Cunningham telegraphed anger, too.

Jayce stuck his head inside DeLong's office and said, "We need to talk, my friend." The tone of his words indicated that he didn't consider the lawman a friend at all. The words came out sounding like a threat.

Jayce came in, sat down on the visitor side of the desk and said, "Who the hell's this Fargo, anyway?"

"He works for your daughter."

"That doesn't answer my question."

Jayce was a massive man and an ugly one. The nose was enormous and had been broken several times. The lips were too big for his face—too big for any face, really. And his left blue eye was slightly crossed. But the worst part of his face was the long purple patch—what they called a port wine stain—on his left cheek. And then there was the beard, so long and full and biblical that you could hide a gun in it if you had to. That was the local joke, anyway. The best that could be said for him was that all of these odds and ends put together gave him a look of ferocity that few could match. He was dressed as usual in what DeLong thought of as funeral clothes—the black suit with the simple white shirt and the black cravat. He said, "Tell me about this Skye Fargo."

DeLong shrugged. "Near as I can figure out, he's a drifter. I have to give him one thing, though. He knew what he was doing when we were looking all around the boathouse where Bonnie's body was. Says he reads up on all the latest things Scotland Yard and the French are doing. I never put much stock in that kind of thing but I can see now where I was wrong."

"And just why the hell is he working for my daughter?"

"Because Helen can't bring herself to believe that her husband's a murderer."

Jayce paused. Looked directly at Harvey. "I don't want this Fargo muddying the waters. We know who the killer is."

"I already promised Helen he could ask around for her."

"Tell her you changed your mind."

"That'd just make things worse, Jayce. She's suspicious enough already. About her husband being guilty, I mean. If I was to pull this Fargo off, she'd start asking a lot more questions."

Every once in a while, DeLong would look at Jayce's cross-eye and almost break out in laughter. But that would be a bad move on his part. Jayce would not forgive him. And Jayce would have his vengeance. And Jayce's vengeance was always ugly and final. DeLong looked away from Jayce's face when he said, "You've got to trust me on this."

"I do, huh? Come into town and I talk to several people and they all tell me how this Fargo's been questioning them. And how they don't like being questioned by strangers. And how they're afraid of this Fargo. And they ask me, 'Mr. Cunningham, isn't there something you can do about this man?' And what am I supposed to tell them? I'm Jayce Cunningham. In their minds there's virtually nothing I can't do. In their minds I'm even stronger than the McLure clan, that's how powerful I am to them. So I come in here and ask you to help me get rid of Fargo and all I get from you is that if we do anything, Helen's going to get suspicious. What do I tell all the people who look up to me, Harvey?"

"It won't be long. I'll see to it that he's finished in twenty-four hours."

Jayce leaned forward in the chair. His unpleasant face was even more unpleasant when he pushed it closer this way. "He can learn a lot in twenty-four hours, Harvey."

"You said you were sure that Theo was the killer. That's good enough for me. And if it's true, then we don't have anything to worry about, do we? Not with Theo sitting in a jail cell back there."

Jayce sighed. "Harvey, I always knew you were a dumb son of a bitch. But I guess I didn't know just *how* dumb until now. Listen to me. I want to know every place this Fargo goes and who he talks to. I want a complete list brought to my house by six o'clock. And in two days, I want him out of town. He can ride out on his own horse or he can go out in a pine box on a railroad car. I don't care which. But I want him gone, you understand me?"

Harvey smiled. "I guess I'm not as dumb as you think, Jayce. I've got a man tailing him and have had since he left my office."

"Well, that's something, anyway."

And that was about as much of a compliment as Harvey was ever going to get from compliment-stingy Jayce Cunningham.

Harvey said, "Jayce, you should relax. We have the bullets and we have Theo in jail. Everything's under control. Fargo doesn't matter anymore."

"You better be right, Harvey. Everything better be under control the way you say it is or I'll run you out of town."

"You're the boss. I know that." There it was again—the sickening tone of a sycophant in his voice. But what choice did he have? Jayce had never been so blunt before, saying he would run Harvey out of town. If that wasn't a threat, what was? Harvey was too old to move on. Plus, as he admitted to himself at certain times, he wasn't that good. He'd never been that good. He'd been fired by two or three towns over the years. Great at glad-handing and walking around with a whole lot of menace on his face. But as for actual competence as a peace officer . . .

Just then a deputy named Thomas Rook knocked on the door and stuck his long, narrow head in the office. He looked as if a giant had placed both hands on either side of Rook's head and began to press inward. The head was just this side of grotesque.

Rook said, "Need to talk to you a minute."

Harvey was astonished. "Rook, Mr. Cunningham is here right now. We'll talk later."

"Oh, right. Hello, Mr. Cunningham."

Jayce didn't turn around to face the man he spoke to. "Hello, Rook. We're a little busy right now."

Even Rook finally caught on. "Say, I didn't mean to interrupt you fellas. I'm sorry about that."

"Fine, Rook," Harvey said. "Now get the hell out of here."

"You bet. I just stopped in to say that I lost that there Fargo fella. But I'm sure I can pick him up later today."

He disappeared from the doorway.

"I can see that you put your best man on the job of following Fargo."

Harvey felt himself blush. That damned dumb Rook. Couldn't even follow a man without losing him. And then standing there blabbing his news in front of one of the men who had the power to fire Harvey, who was too old to go anyplace else if he got let go here.

"I'm putting my next man on it. My number two."

"Given the caliber of your men—and I include you in this, Harvey—that isn't all that reassuring."

Harvey had to restrain himself from reaching over the desk and grabbing Jayce by the front of his expensive shirt and then slapping the hell out of him for an hour or so.

"There's no call for that, Jayce."

Jayce laughed. "No call for that? Harvey, the man you put on the job is a damned dunce. His clothes, his manner, his speaking voice—he's a rube. And you hired him. If you had competent men, they could tell us where this Fargo is right now."

"I can find out, Jayce. Don't worry, I won't let you down."

Jayce stood up. "You damned well hadn't *better* let me down, Harvey. You got that straight?"

Harvey was flushed again—anger, resentment, shame. God, he hated Jayce Cunningham.

"You understand me, Harvey?"

"Yes, Jayce," Harvey said with great weariness. "I understand."

14

Fargo had to give DeLong's deputies one thing: they were relentless. This new one was probably about Fargo's age, but otherwise that was the only resemblance—where Fargo was muscular, slim and black-haired—an air of the panther about him that several women had remarked on over the years—this man was chunky, slow-footed and gray-haired. Only his face spoke of his true age. He looked as young as Fargo, though the expression he wore was melancholy, even sad.

He'd started following Fargo as soon as the Trailsman had left the bank. Fargo stopped for some tobacco and papers and to get a better look at the deputy who wasn't exactly a wizard at trailing somebody. Twice, he peeked in the front window of the tobacco shop. Fargo got a clear look at his face.

Fargo looked through magazines, talked a bit with the counterman about how the whole town was startled by the arrest of Theo Mason. Nothing like this, said the counterman, had ever happened here before, and the common people didn't quite know what to make of it because ordinarily the rich folks stuck together. And this had happened right on top of old man McLure being murdered in his own study by one of his most trusted ranch hands.

When he walked out of the tobacco shop, Fargo turned and looked directly at the deputy and said, "I'm going to have lunch with that beautiful woman who works at the bank. I'm sure you know the one I mean. Would you like to join us? I'm sure she wouldn't mind."

The deputy failed to see the humor in Fargo's gibe.

"You're in a lot more trouble than you think. I'd keep that in mind."

"Oh? Is that what Harvey's saying about me now?"

"You don't want to cross him, mister. And you've crossed him plenty already."

"He should send all you deputies to Denver. They've got a good police school there. They could teach you a lot about shadowing somebody."

"He said you were a wiseacre."

Fargo laughed. "Well, I suppose he was right about that. But since you're not joining us for lunch, you may as well go back to the marshal's office and relax for forty minutes or so. She's only got forty-five minutes and you can make it to the café down the street in five. You can start following me again after lunch."

"You know something, mister?"

"I can tell I'm not going to like this."

"You're a gen-u-ine A-number-one asshole."

And with that, the deputy stormed off.

"Simone Callahan," the redhead told him. "My mother was French and my father was Irish."

" 'Was'?"

"They had a little scrub farm up on the river. Right in the middle of the Indian wars about six years ago. I was still a teenager. I'd come to town to see how my aunt was doing. She was always very sickly and my mother worried about her constantly. Mom had to help with the crops so she sent me to town. While I was gone the Indians raided the place and killed my folks. So don't ask me my opinion of Indians because you won't be able to shut me up."

"Well, there are good ones and bad ones, the same as any other group."

"I guess I just met the bad ones."

The serving woman came with their food. They were both eating beef and large buttered slices of wheat bread.

After they'd eaten silently for a time, Fargo said, "Do you know Mason well?"

An impishness came into her lovely brown eyes. "Not as well as he'd like me to know him. I actually like him.

He's a charming man. But I don't want to be just another one of his conquests. Plus he's married. I like his wife. She's one of the few rich women in this town who treats me like I'm an actual human being."

"But you know him well enough to say that he's not a killer. What about the gun they found?"

"Guns can always be planted."

"I was thinking that myself. That's why I didn't get too excited when they found it."

"When Theo's had too much to drink, he likes to act tough. But he's not tough. Plus, Bonnie had him wrapped around her little finger. The only thing he could do to prove his dignity was to cheat on her. And then he'd always come crawling back and beg for forgiveness."

"So he was cheating on both his wife and his mistress?"

"I guess you could put it that way, though I'd hate to call Bonnie his 'mistress' to her face. She'd—or would have when she was alive anyway—claw your eyes out."

"You wouldn't happen to have any idea who might have killed her, would you?"

She surprised him. "Sure. The same person a lot of people think killed her."

"And who would that be?"

"Her brother, David."

"David? But why would he do that?"

"Because he stood to inherit everything with her gone. And because he was sick of the scandal. He'd tried breaking them up several times. He even gave Theo a pretty good beating one night and warned him to stay away from his sister. But it didn't do any good. It may have been a scandal but those two couldn't keep their hands off each other."

"That's kind of funny."

"What is?"

"He was my first guess, too. Just something about him."

"He's a real prig, as I told you. So you have the scandal. Plus he's more ruthless than his father ever was. He's driven by power—wanting more and more of it."

"Maybe I should have a talk with him. By the way, do you get a break this afternoon?"

"Yes, at two thirty, because I have to work until five. I could meet you here."

She did it then—touched one of her breasts in that slow, erotic way she had in the bank. "I hope I'll be seeing you tonight, too."

"They don't mind if you have men in your room?"

"The landlady is very old and very deaf. I could have a big party there and she'd never hear it."

"That's a nice setup." He stood up. "C'mon, I'll walk you back to work."

Fargo knew that in any serious investigation of a crime you didn't concentrate all your efforts on the most likely suspect. Right now that person was David McLure, but that was only because he stood to inherit the entire McLure estate. That made him a good suspect but it didn't make him a murderer.

These were his thoughts as he approached the one-story redbrick building that sat near the courthouse. CUNNINGHAM ASSOCIATES read the scrollwork above the front door.

Inside, confronted by a middle-aged woman at the front desk, he said, "I'd like to see Mr. Cunningham." She had been clattering away on one of those newfangled typewriters. She stopped now, her dark dismissive eyes obviously not taken with the man standing in front of her.

"Do you have an appointment?"

"I'm afraid not."

"Then seeing Mr. Cunningham is impossible."

"I have some information about Theo Mason he might find interesting."

For the first time, she seemed to really focus on him. She didn't seem to like him any better. But at least now he had her serious attention.

"And what would that information be, exactly?"

Fargo glanced around the large, open reception area. Framed photographs of Cunningham with various dignitaries covered the walls. Cunningham had obviously brought his own photographer along. He was always the largest figure in every photograph, giving the impression that he was more important than any of the mere mortals he came across.

"I can only tell Mr. Cunningham."

"Then I'm afraid I can't let you see him."

Fargo said, "You know how mad he's going to be if he finds out you didn't tell him about me? It could mean your job."

"I doubt that." But Fargo could see the doubt in her eyes now. Doubt and confusion. She didn't want to bother her temperamental boss with somebody who had no right seeing him. But what if this stranger was telling the truth—that he actually had useful information for Mr. Cunningham? And what if Mr. Cunningham later learned that she had turned the stranger away?

"I don't even know your name," she said, fingering the old-lady brooch that sat in the midst of her frilly white collar.

"It's Fargo, ma'am. Skye Fargo."

She allowed her frustration to show. "I'm just not sure what to do here."

"I won't need much time. Five minutes at the outside."

"Really? It could be that short?"

"It sure could. And will be."

"Well, I suppose—" She stood up for the first time, smoothed down the long, green dress she wore. "Let me tell him you're here."

"I appreciate this."

"I just hope you don't get me in trouble."

"I don't want to get either one of us in trouble, ma'am."

She leaned toward him, spoke in a whisper. "You don't know what he's like when he's mad."

"How often is he mad?"

She had a nice smile. "Twenty-four hours a day." Then she nodded to his holster and Colt. "You'll have to leave your gun out here. If he'll agree to see you, I mean."

"I'm sure he'll have a gun."

"Those are the rules."

Fargo shrugged. "Fine."

She went away and was back in a few minutes. She looked surprised. "He said of course he'd see you."

"I figured he would."

"And why would you figure that?"

"Just a feeling I had." Fargo didn't add, *Probably wants to get a look at me before he has one of his gunnies kill me.*

She led him back through a wide hallway. She knocked on a massive oak door and when a grunt came from the other side, she leaned down, took the knob in her hand and swept the door open with a certain dramatic flair, as if she was offering Fargo his first look at God.

And godlike Cunningham was, as he sat behind a massive desk that was set upon about two feet of platform beneath. The second thing Fargo noticed was that there were no chairs. All visitors stood.

"Good day to you, Mr. Fargo," Cunningham said. With his biblical beard and his booming voice, he did have a presence that set him apart from most other human beings. But where others might find him intimidating, Fargo had a different feeling about the man. And it was a familiar feeling, too, one that Fargo had known throughout his years of traveling the country. Cunningham was a killer. No amount of money, no amount of social skills, no amount of seeming goodwill could quite disguise the man's basic nature. If he wanted something from you and couldn't get it—information, compliance—he'd kill you for it. And he'd have no regrets.

He spoke first. "Harvey tells me you're working for my daughter."

"I am."

"Well, I want to thank you."

He's a crafty bastard, Fargo thought. *Instead of going right at me and telling me to get out of town, he tries to get on my good side.*

"I'm kind of surprised by that."

"That I wanted to thank you? Listen, Theo is one of my favorite people. Or was until he killed Bonnie and her father. Now I need to protect my daughter. I know you showed Harvey up at the boathouse. Had everybody check over the whole place just the way they did in those articles you told them about. Well, that's all well and good, but in the end Harvey came up with a lot more proof than you ever did."

"If you mean Theo's gun, that could have been planted. I wonder why Theo would use a gun that could be traced so easy."

Cunningham sat back in his chair, steepled his fingers. "Now we were getting along so fine and dandy here. I was understanding you and I hoped you were understanding me. And then you had to go and ruin it, didn't you?"

"Just stating my opinion."

"Well, what if I also told you that I don't appreciate you challenging the word of our duly elected town marshal? A man every single one of the important people in this town trusts the way they do their own flesh and blood."

"And the man you own lock, stock and barrel."

Cunningham smirked. "You sound bound and determined to get yourself killed in this town, Mr. Fargo. And my feeling is we've had enough of that in this town. I'd sure hate to keep going on a streak like this. I don't want to live in a town with a reputation like that. Nobody does."

This was the civic mask Cunningham wore on special occasions when he was playing Public Citizen. The ferocity of his face worked against his words. He was still a dark and murderous figure no matter what his words suggested.

"For your sake, Mr. Fargo—now that I've met you— I think what you should do is quietly tell Helen that you've decided to move on. That you can't help her. That you think Theo may be guilty after all. And then you know what I'd do?"

He didn't wait for Fargo to answer.

"I'd get on that horse of yours and ride out of here. There are some fine inns along the eastern passage. You could be at one of them by sundown if you left in an hour or so. You'd find good grub and a good bed for a long night's sleep. And you wouldn't have to worry about getting yourself killed."

"You make that sound very pleasant, Cunningham. But you're forgetting something."

"Oh—and what would that be?"

"That I'd be leaving Theo Mason behind. Right now I don't know for sure if he's guilty or not. But I owe it to Helen to find out."

"And you owe it to yourself, Mr. Fargo, to stay alive."

Fargo smiled. "You're not very subtle about your threats."

"Over the years, I've learned that subtlety doesn't usually get you anywhere. You have to make yourself clear on the subject. And from what I've said, you couldn't prove that I was threatening you, Mr. Fargo. That's the conclusion you drew from my words, not me. I was simply giving you friendly advice."

He reached over and took his watch from his vest pocket. "We're out of time, Mr. Fargo. You've had your say and I've had mine. I hope you're sensible enough to take my advice. Like I say, this town has had enough killing. Good day, now."

Fargo nodded and left.

15

Fargo sat in the café. He was ten minutes early to meet Simone on her break. He worked on a cup of steaming black coffee. He also worked on a scrap of paper listing his suspects.

David McLure—inherit entire estate
Jayce Cunningham—bring down the McLure empire
Glen Davis—jealousy
Theo Mason—Bonnie pushing him to divorce Helen

This was something he'd learned from a most fetching and definitely female Pinkerton he'd met one time in Omaha. She had been working on a year-old murder case that the locals hadn't been able to solve. She solved it in three days. Fargo had paid close attention to how she'd worked, made some of her methods his own.

Listing suspects and motives was helpful. You could add or subtract names as the investigation proceeded. And it kept everything clear for you.

He was just about to fold his list and put it in his pocket when he saw a large man in a black funeral suit come in the front door and walk directly over to him.

The man was a good six-four with a face that looked as if it had known a good deal of violence over the years, showing Fargo that for all his swagger, the man wasn't as formidable as he appeared. With his size, his face shouldn't look like this. He made no secret of the six-shooter he carried.

"Stand up."

It was a nice clean café, small tables and booths sparkling in the autumn sunlight splashing through the front windows. The only other customers at this time of the afternoon were a pair of ladies in big imposing show hats sitting in a booth far back.

Fargo hated the thought of messing the café up.

"I said stand up."

"You look like you've been worked over a lot for a guy your size."

"When you're my size, they use anything they can on you. Ball bats, pickax handles, scrap pieces of lumber. That's how I got banged up this way."

"Sad story. I'd cry but it's too early for me. I only cry at night."

"C'mon, up on your feet. We're wastin' time."

Fargo knew how he was going to handle this. Or try handling it anyway. You never knew how things were going to turn out. He'd need luck to pull it off. But the big man might be luckier at this particular moment and manage to kill Fargo after all.

Fargo stood up.

"Put that Colt on the table."

Fargo complied. The big man picked it up. Now he had one gun for each hand.

The woman working behind the counter must have recognized that the big man worked for Jayce Cunningham. She strained very hard not to notice—or seem to notice—anything that was going on. Did the big man have a gun pointed at the man who'd been quietly sitting at the table by himself? She didn't notice. Was the big man now marching the other man toward the front door at gunpoint? Didn't seem to notice that, either.

She even tried not to notice what Fargo managed to pull off as he got near the front door.

The big man's obvious plan was to march Fargo out the front door and walk him out into the fields that surrounded the northern part of town and kill him there. The dogs and the birds would find him fast but it would take a while before humans found the corpse. Harvey would launch one of his world-famous investigations and would either never solve it or run in some drunk as his man. Four, five months from now the man would hang for the murder of Skye Fargo, the real killer walking around free.

Fargo had other plans.

When he reached the door, he threw himself to the left of the doorframe, then grabbed the edge of the door and slammed it in the face of the big man. The man fired, of course, and the two shots were enough to stop street traffic. Humans and horses alike were immediately alert to the dreaded sound of gunfire.

Fargo went after the big man now, grabbing his wrist before another round could be fired, twisting it so savagely that the crack of bone was almost as loud as the bullets had been.

Fargo now saw what accounted for the man's battered face. While his size was intimidating and his six-gun even more so, the man was no threat without firepower. He was slow and clumsy and now, with a broken wrist, he was totally worthless as a fighter. He was sobbing loudly. Not a good thing for a supposed tough guy to do.

Fargo leaned down, took back his own gun, then emptied the big man's gun, stuffing the man's ammunition in his own pocket.

Just then he saw the sexy sight of Simone Callahan coming up the street toward the café. This was no place to take a lady.

"Sorry for all the trouble, ma'am," he said to the woman behind the counter. She'd just carried four loaves of fresh bread from the back. The smell was good, homey.

"I'm just glad to see him get a little bit of his own medicine, mister. With Jayce backin' him, he thinks he can do anything he wants and get away with it. If we had a real town marshal, he'd have been in prison a long time ago."

Simone was in the doorway now. She looked down at the big man writhing on the floor and then she smiled at Fargo. "Do you make friends everywhere you go?"

"I try to," Fargo laughed. Then he took her arm and gently guided her out onto the sidewalk. "Maybe we'd better find another café."

She was still amused. "Yes, that seems to be a sensible

idea. We don't want to be here when Jayce's backup men get here."

"What's that man's name anyway, the one on the floor?"

"You mean you don't know?"

"Huh-uh. Should I?"

"Skye, you just broke the wrist of Jayce's one and only son—Jayce Jr. And Jayce is not going to be happy at all."

"Well, I never was all that good at making friends."

"I'm glad you think this is funny."

Fargo shook his head. "It's not good news, I'm not saying that. But given all the trouble I'm in already, it's just one more problem."

"You'll be lucky if they don't shoot you."

"Just as long as they hold off till I prove that Theo didn't kill Bonnie McLure."

"Helen," she said. "Men get very protective of her. I can see you have, too."

"Maybe. But more than anything, I want to prove to this town that they can break the hold that Harvey and his backers have on them. This is one killing that's going to get solved right. I'm pretty sure that whoever killed old man McLure also killed Bonnie. I don't have any evidence of it yet but that's the idea I'm working on. It's just too coincidental otherwise."

They found another café. This one affected a Parisian air, which, Fargo reasoned, must appeal to about ten percent of a cowboy town like this one.

Fargo and Simone ordered coffee. Across from them a rather fussy-looking man said to his woman, "I wish you'd learn French someday, Delores. Then I wouldn't have to order for you all the time."

Simone laughed softly. "What a priss. The waiter here doesn't speak French, either."

"Then if the man orders in French, how does he know what the priss is ordering?"

"He always has the man point to the right place on the menu. The priss knows he doesn't speak French. He just likes to hear himself speak a foreign language."

"My kind of folks."

"Yeah, I'll bet."

Over their coffee, Fargo said, "Tell me about Theo's enemies."

"We'd need three lunchtimes for that."

"Really? That many?"

"He's a banker, Skye. That means he has to turn people down for loans, order foreclosures, even drag people into court sometimes. He has a list of enemies that probably reaches a hundred or so."

"Anybody ever try and kill him?"

"A drunken man came into the bank once and held a gun to his head. I thought for sure Theo would die right then and there. But I didn't give him credit enough for his charm. He talked the gun out of the man's hand and then took him across the street for a good meal and a pot of coffee. He didn't press charges, either. He's only violent when he gets drunk—and then he's not very good at it."

Fargo said, "He was holding his own against Bonnie the first time I saw him."

She laughed. "Well, yes, Bonnie he could probably beat up. But not a man." She glanced at the clock on the wall. "This has gone by too fast for me. I hate to go back." She reached over and touched his hand. "But we'll have more time tonight."

After leaving Simone, Fargo walked over to the livery. Halfway there, he saw an argument going on between two people he recognized instantly—Helen Mason and David McLure. Other people saw it, too. A small crowd had gathered in the dusty street to listen in, the crowd a mixture of clerks, merchants, cowhands, housewives and a few early-day drunks who'd spilled out of the nearby saloons to see what all the fuss was about.

"I can't help it, Helen," McLure said. "You know deep down that your husband killed my sister. I know the whole thing's hard for you to talk about—they carried on right in front of everybody, including you and me—and things got out of hand and he killed her."

"He didn't kill her," Helen shot back. "Theo couldn't kill anybody."

"When he was drunk and mad, he could. And that's

what he did, came out to the boathouse for a prearranged meeting and killed her. I'm not saying he planned it, Helen. I don't want to see him charged with first-degree murder. But he has to stand trial for second-degree or maybe even manslaughter. He's guilty of that at the very least. In a way, my sister's behavior probably brought all this on."

Fargo stood on the edge of the crowd. Every time he saw McLure he liked him less. Talking down your own flesh and blood in public was a singularly ugly thing to do. Whatever her faults, Bonnie deserved some brother-sister loyalty. But she wasn't going to get it from this prig of a man.

"If Harvey wasn't so lazy and so stupid, he'd be out looking for the real culprit right now," Helen said. "My husband doesn't belong in jail."

McLure shook his head as if in great misery. "I don't know how you can stick up for him, Helen, after he humiliated you in front of everybody."

"Because I love him, that's why I can stick up for him."

McLure snorted. "I doubt Theo's worth your love."

The slap came so fast and so hard, nobody was prepared for it, least of all McLure.

Slender though she was, Helen was able to rock the man back on the heels of his boots. "Don't ever say anything against my husband again, not to me. Tell your lies to everybody else but leave me out of them."

McLure looked angry enough to slap her right back. His hand favored the red-splotched handprint she'd left on the right side of his face. "I feel sorry for you, Helen. You're a good woman. You deserve a lot better life than you've had." He glanced around, as if seeing the crowd for the first time. "They're taking a lot of pleasure in this. They love to see the rich people fight. They don't care that we're both in agony here."

"I'm not in agony because I know my husband's name will be cleared. It's only a matter of time."

McLure's gaze now settled on Fargo. He scoffed. "Because Fargo's helping you?" He shook his head again. "Oh, Helen, don't get involved with people like him.

He's some drifter who's out to take your money and nothing else. Just because he's read up on some modern police techniques—"

Fargo walked over to stand next to Helen. "You want to tell me to my face that I'm stealing her money, McLure? You have guts enough to do it?"

"What're you going to do, Fargo, shoot me? I expect that's how you settle most of your arguments, isn't it?"

"You'll find out if you don't take back what you just said about me."

McLure, used to being in control of every situation, realized that he didn't want a fight with this man. McLure was no coward but he wasn't a fool, either. You didn't get into a fight with a man who was so obviously your superior. At the least, you'd get a thrashing. At worst, you'd be dead.

"You're right, Fargo. I shouldn't have said that. I don't know it for a fact. But I'm worried about Helen here. She's had enough misery already and—"

"Don't speak for me, McLure. I despise you." She slid her arm through Fargo's and said, "Will you walk me home?"

"Sure, be glad to."

As they left, Fargo took a last look at McLure. The man wasn't used to apologizing. Fargo had backed him off in front of a crowd that had never seen a McLure in this situation before. A McLure apologize to a commoner? Unthinkable.

"I've always hated him," Helen said. "He's so pontifical. He acts like he's the Lord himself. But he's just as ruthless as his father was."

"How did the argument start today?"

"He came up to me and said there should be no hard feelings. And that in fact it was maybe a good thing that Theo had been arrested. Then I could divorce him and start my life again. Can you imagine the arrogance of that?"

"I take it he and Theo had had some run-ins about Bonnie."

"I didn't know about any of them until yesterday. A neighbor told me that she'd seen the two of them in a shoving match downtown. And she'd heard of other times they'd argued in public."

They had reached her block. She stopped him with her hand and turned to him. "You still believe me, don't you, Skye? That Theo's innocent?"

He was afraid she was going to cry. "I'm taking your word for it, Helen. But I'm hoping to prove it to myself to be sure. The big thing now is to connect those two murders. Old man McLure and Bonnie McLure."

Frown lines wrinkled her forehead. "You're sure they're connected?"

"All I've got to go on right now is my instinct. And my instinct tells me that whoever killed one killed the other."

She fought back tears. "I just want Theo home again."

"I'll do everything I can to help, Helen. Right now maybe you need a rest."

She smiled, the old Helen, the friendly one. "Before I lose my mind and you start thinking I'm this old harpy."

"I think you know better than that. You just need to try and put this out of your mind for a while."

"Right now what sounds good is a cup of cocoa and something good to read. That should help."

"Good. And I'll get in touch with you as soon as there's more news."

She squeezed his arm. "Thank God you're here to help me, Skye. I'd never make it through without you."

"You're a strong woman, Helen. You'd make it just fine without me."

He walked her the rest of the way to her imposing house. The wealthy did live well in this town, no doubt about it. A Mexican man was raking her leaves, smiling at her from beneath his wide straw hat. In the back, leaves were burning in a large pile. The smoke was as heady as the most seductive perfume.

"Thanks, Skye."

"My pleasure."

He watched her until she reached the front door and then he turned back to town.

16

Six steps from his hotel room door, Fargo heard a noise that stopped him. Somebody was inside his room, moving about furtively. Looking for something.

Fargo drew his Colt and moved forward carefully. He put his ear to the door, listened. Whoever was tossing his room was an amateur. A professional would hold the noise to a minimum.

Fargo grabbed the doorknob and flung the door inward. By the time Jayce Jr. had time to turn around, it was too late to pull his own gun. Fargo said, "Throw the gun on the bed. And right now."

The massive man shook his head like a child who'd been caught doing something nasty. He probably wasn't used to taking orders from a drifter. He obviously resented it. As yet, he hadn't said a word. But he did toss his gun on the bed.

Fargo closed the door behind him. "What're you looking for?"

"I wasn't looking for anything."

Fargo smiled. "Just got my room by mistake, huh?"

"Yeah, somethin' like that."

Fargo crossed to the bigger man with three steps. He cracked the man across the jaw with his gun barrel. Jayce Jr., big as he was, started to fold up from the sudden pain. His knees gave out. He fell back against the wall.

Not much doubt about what he was doing here, Fargo knew. They hadn't been able to get rid of him any other way so Jayce and Harvey had sent Jayce Jr. to steal something from Fargo's room—something that would be left behind at a murder scene. They wouldn't be stupid enough to murder anybody important, just some transient who happened to be passing through. And next to his corpse would be something of Fargo's. Something that would be "proof" that he was the killer. And then Fargo would be in jail and on his way through a system that would lead to the gallows eventually. All perfectly legal.

"Empty your pockets."

"Why should I?"

"Empty your pockets or you get slugged again and this time I won't hold back."

For all his size, the big man was a nervous sort. His useless right hand hung by his side. His left hand trembled now as he reached into the pocket of his black suit coat. He pulled the pocket inside out. Nothing. He went through each pocket, including the two back ones on his black trousers, turning each out for Fargo to see. As he neared the last one, he started smiling, as if he'd beaten Fargo at a game. The only thing he'd been carrying, apparently, was a silver money clip fat with green.

And then Fargo said, "Inside your suit coat."

"What?"

"You heard me."

"There isn't anything in there."

"Open your coat and turn that pocket inside out. The way you did with the rest of them."

Jayce Jr. sighed, unhappy about complying. But just as he opened his coat, he ducked down and sprang awkwardly at Fargo. He'd jumped fast enough that Fargo couldn't get off a clean shot. His size alone made him difficult to handle as he shoved Fargo back against the door. His huge left hand went immediately to Fargo's gun hand.

But that was as far as he got. Fargo was mad at himself for not anticipating what Jayce Jr. had done. He took a lot of it out on the punches he landed on the side of Jayce's face.

The final punch landed on Jayce's ear. That one not only staggered him, it forced him back two steps. But Fargo didn't stop. He continued to slam punches into the other man's face and head until Jayce collapsed with a bloody nose and the makings of a big round shiner on his right eye.

Jayce was unconscious. Fargo wasted no time. He shoved his hand inside the pocket of Jayce's suit coat. He found an old railroad ticket with his name written on it. They weren't subtle in this town. No doubt about who the killer was when your name was written on a ticket next to a corpse.

He grabbed Jayce Jr. by the collar of his suit coat and dragged him out into the hallway. A pair of startled drummers watched as Fargo propped the unconscious man up against the wall.

"He's just a little tired is all," Fargo said.

Then he closed his door and picked up the new sack of tobacco he'd come here for.

He left Jayce Jr. in the hallway, knocked out and about to wake up with one hell of a headache.

As he left the hotel, Fargo saw a familiar face driving an expensive buggy toward the mortuary. David McLure. McLure's wife sat next to him. Not far behind them came the outsized surrey he'd seen yesterday, the one belonging to Jayce Cunningham Sr. And behind Cunningham, on horseback, came Glen Davis. Each man was dressed in black, appropriate for a funeral home visit. McLure's wife wore not only a black dress but also a small black hat with a veil.

On the steps of the one-story adobe mortuary stood a preacher with a Bible clutched to his chest. He watched as each guest walked toward him. He had words for each of them.

And then the biggest surprise of all. Even though he'd told her to stay home and rest, Helen Mason, also dressed in black, came down the walk. She stopped in front of the funeral home. Even from here Fargo could see that the preacher was startled by her showing up. If anybody had had the right to hate Bonnie McLure, it was surely Helen Mason.

Fargo waited until they were all inside and then he crossed the street and went into the building himself.

The air was suffocating with the heavy scents of fresh flowers and incense. From the back there was even a slight aroma of the fluid morticians used to prepare the corpses for burial.

A heavy rumble of voices could be heard on the other side of the divided doors that had been rolled together. The minister led everyone in prayers. This wasn't the time to interrupt. Fargo waited until the prayers were over and then he went up to the doors and pushed them open.

The minister stood in front of an open coffin. The mourners formed a group in front of him. The minister had apparently handed out prayer sheets because each mourner held a single sheet of paper. David McLure's wife was wiping tears from her eyes.

They turned to look at Fargo with great scorn. "This is a private ceremony," David McLure snapped. "I'd appreciate it if you'd leave."

"And I'd appreciate it if you'd tell me which one of you killed her—and killed your father."

Fargo had seen touring companies that did mystery plays where all the suspects were gathered in a single room. This was a similar situation. He felt sure that one of the people here was the murderer.

He nodded to Glen Davis. "You hated her because she betrayed you." He looked at Jayce Cunningham. "You wanted to take care of Theo Mason. Framing him for murder would be the best way to do it. You'd humiliate him and then watch him go to prison for the rest of his life." And then he turned to David McLure. "And with your father and your sister out of the way, you have the power and the money you've always wanted."

The minister stepped forward and said, "This is a sacred occasion. We're holding a wake for a soul that has left us. You have no right to intrude this way."

"I'm after a killer," Fargo said. "That's the best way I know to honor her—to find out who really killed her."

Jayce Cunningham made a fist and shook it in Fargo's direction. "By God, man, I swear I'll see you in prison or on the gallows. You've disrupted this whole town." He turned to Helen and said, "I know you're afraid, Helen. But for right now just accept the fact that Theo's been charged. He's safe in his cell. Nothing's going to happen to him. If he's not guilty, we'll find out." He

111

appeared more biblical than ever, sunlight streaming through a nearby window highlighting the fierce blackness of his huge beard.

"In other words, Father," Helen said, "I just sit and watch while my husband gets railroaded. I don't know whose idea it was to blame Theo but I agree with Skye—it's one of you people here—David or Glen or you yourself, Father."

Now it was David McLure's turn. His suddenly mottled cheeks spoke to his rage. "That's a damned lie, Helen. Nobody put anybody up to anything. If your husband hadn't been cavorting around with my sister—well, I don't have to be any clearer, do I? You know the situation as well as I do."

"Yes, I do know the situation, David. Your sister was a very loose woman."

McLure made an ugly face. "Get out of here, Helen! You don't belong here and you weren't invited." He pointed to the door. "Take this drifter you're so fond of and go bother somebody else. We're trying to mourn my sister here. Whatever else she was, she was my little sister and I loved her. And I want this wake to be respectful. Now get out!"

Jayce Cunningham raised a fist and said, "Don't talk to my daughter that way. She's only talking crazy because her husband's in jail."

"The cause of all this trouble is Fargo," McLure shouted. "He put all these thoughts in her head."

McLure stepped forward as if he was going to swing on Fargo but the minister, a dumpy man in a black suit that showed stains from tobacco and meals alike, hurried between them.

"That would be the worst thing of all—violence here on top of the violence that took Bonnie's life. Now you two behave like gentlemen for the sake of everybody here."

Helen Mason was suddenly at Fargo's side. She took his hand and said, "C'mon, Skye, walk me outside."

"You shouldn't have been here, anyway," snapped Glen Davis.

"I came because I'm sorry she's dead. I thought it was

the right thing to do." Helen showed the strain of the past few days. She looked older now, almost wan.

Fargo led her out into the hall and then outside. He was happy to breathe fresh air again. He'd felt suffocated in the mortuary.

"I was just trying to show that I forgave her," Helen said. Then she grimaced. "Actually, I wasn't being all that noble, Skye. I thought maybe I'd help Theo's case if I went in there and showed my face. Showed that we had nothing to hide."

"You weren't any more popular than I was."

"McLure is so sanctimonious. I thought I was going to choke once he started making speeches. He's always been that way."

"I'm going to spend some time finding out about his fishing trip."

"You think there's something there?"

"I'm just checking out alibis. Glen Davis, Jayce Cunningham and McLure. It's going to be a long day."

"They'll be after you for sure now, Skye. After the funeral home, I mean."

Fargo didn't respond, just took her arm and escorted her up the street.

"You go get some rest, Helen. You're looking pretty tired."

"Not my usual ravishing self, Skye?" She laughed at herself. "If only I'd been as vivacious as Bonnie McLure. Maybe none of this would have happened."

This is a woman who blames herself for everything, Fargo thought. *Her husband cheats on her and somehow it's her fault.*

But all he said was, "Get some rest."

He reckoned he had about an hour to get to Glen Davis' ranch before Davis got out of the funeral home and showed up there himself. Fargo put his stallion to work. It was another clear, bright autumn day, with the leaves resplendent in their burnished colors and the river noisy with boats of all sizes.

Davis' spread was a modest one that stretched from a line of timber to gently sloping foothills. The house on it was small but new. The windows threw back the sunlight with remarkable diamondlike clarity. Cattle surrounded the spread on three sides. Five cowhands were busy branding a dozen head of cattle, a practice, Fargo had read, that went way back to ancient Egypt. He'd done his share of branding from time to time. Sometimes the life of a cowpoke appealed to him. But then the wanderlust always came on him and he was off to distant places.

Fargo surveyed Glen Davis' operation.

The relatively small size of the cattle ranch was due to the problem of overstocking that had two years ago put a number of ranches into bankruptcy. They'd had more stock than they knew what to do with and when winter came six weeks early, bringing with it savage blizzards, thousands of cattle died. The ranchers had invested all their money in excess stock. They knew better now, having learned the lesson the hard way.

Now Glen Davis had a nice, sensible-sized spread here, one with nearby streams, nutritious grasses that were good for winter grazing, and coulees and ravines that provided shelter for the animals.

One of the cowboys watched Fargo ride up. The man eased his six-shooter from his holster, letting it dangle free from his fingers but obviously ready to use it if need be.

The other men moved to form a semicircle behind their coworker. They'd be grateful for something to break up the monotony of the day. Here was a stranger to have a little fun with. Or so they thought anyway.

Fargo approached cautiously. He raised a hand in greeting and said, "Would Glen Davis happen to be here?"

None of the men responded.

Fargo rode closer. "I'm not here for any trouble, men. I'm just trying to help somebody out. Her husband's in a lot of trouble."

Still the faces remained solemn, unfriendly, silent.

"We know who you are," the man with the six-shooter said.

As Fargo dropped from his stallion, the man said,

"You're that Fargo, ain't ya?" The man was thin but had a hard look about him.

"Watch yourself with him, Ned," a beefy man said while gnawing on a cigar.

"You need that gun, do you?" Fargo asked him.

"All depends on what you're doing here."

"Like I said, I'm trying to help somebody whose husband is in trouble."

"You ain't no lawman."

"True enough. But that doesn't mean I can't lend a hand since the lawman in this town doesn't see fit to do anything the carriage trade doesn't tell him to do."

"We don't want you here, mister. And that means that if you're smart you'll be gone in about sixty seconds."

The threat in Ned's voice tensed up everybody standing behind him. The prospect of violence was getting better all the time. Who wanted to miss a good fight? And this crowd obviously wanted to see some action.

"Just wanted to ask you if you remember where your boss was when Bonnie McLure was killed."

The man's face split into a cold grin. "Oh, that's right. I heard you was workin' for Helen Mason. You tryin' to pin it on Glen, are you?"

One of the other men laughed. "That'd be all right with me. You take Glen and hang him. And I'll be one happy man."

They all laughed then.

Ned took a step closer to Fargo. His hand hadn't left his gun. "But as far as me helping you mess up his alibi—won't do it, Fargo. I don't much like him but he pays fair and he pays prompt. Those are hard things to come by these days." He glanced over his shoulder at the other men. "And I think all the boys would like you to leave now."

"Two people are dead. Guess you don't mind if the wrong man gets convicted or not?"

"If you mean Theo Mason—hell, no. If he's not guilty of this he's plenty guilty of other things—namely, sleeping with half the married women in town. That makes him a lot of enemies."

"Bonnie McLure had an enemy, too—your boss. He

didn't take it very well when he found out what she was doing behind his back, did he?"

"That wouldn't be any of your business, Fargo."

"I'm just trying to get the truth."

"Look, I'll tell you one thing, wherever the boss says he was, he was. Far as I know, he was at the Bar D. And anyway, you're startin' to get on my nerves."

And then Ned made his mistake. Instead of just inviting Fargo to leave, he gave Fargo a shove. And Fargo shoved right back. Ned would have gone over backward but a pair of his friends got their hands under his back and kept him upright.

"You just made a bad mistake, Fargo."

"The mistake was yours. And I hope you're not stupid enough to make another one."

But it was too late for words. The man swung hard and wide, catching Fargo along the side of the jaw. But it wasn't a clean punch so Fargo was able to shrug it off and make his own move. His left fist knifed deep into the man's stomach, and when the man doubled over, Fargo clubbed him with a right hand that staggered him even more than the body punch had.

Ned tried to right himself but all he could do was stumble forward a few feet, swinging crazily as he did so.

"C'mon, Ned, give it to him," somebody in the crowd yelled. "Just hit him with that right hand of yours."

"He hits him good with that right hand," another man said, "Fargo's finished."

Ned used these moments well. He gathered himself. His eyes came back into focus, he stood upright and his breathing settled into its normal pattern. He put his fists up the way bare-knuckled fighters did and then proceeded to circle around Fargo.

He got in two good punches, Fargo had to admit. One was a surprise left that connected with Fargo's jaw and jolted him for a minute. Now it was Fargo's eyes that went out of focus for a few moments. The other punch was a hooking right that caught Fargo in the ribs. This, too, staggered Fargo. The cowhands started shouting encouragement now, calling for Ned to finish Fargo.

"I'll buy the beer all night if you put Fargo away!" somebody shouted.

"I'll buy you a bottle of good whiskey!" somebody else promised.

This was when Ned made another mistake. He got so exhilarated with the cheers that he glanced over to see his friends. He smiled at them, clearly feeling that he had everything under control now.

Fargo hit him on the right side of the face with such force that Ned was lifted off the ground. Then Fargo attacked. Nobody could keep count of the number of lefts and rights that Fargo pounded into Ned's upper body and face. One sure gauge of how the fight was going was the sudden silence among the cowpokes. There was nothing to cheer now.

Ned wobbled backward. Fargo followed him, lashing at him with fists that worked with machinelike precision.

This time, the man fell to his knees and then spilled forward and hit the ground with his face. But the fight wasn't over. A pair of cowhands came at Fargo with knives. Being outnumbered this way meant that Fargo had to equal things out quickly. He yanked his Colt from its holster and leveled it right at the cowhand approaching from the left. "I can't fight all of you here. But if you make one more move, I'm killing you on the spot, you understand?"

"C'mon, Tim. Let's move in on the bastard."

But Tim, the chunky man on the left, understood that Fargo was serious. He'd drop Tim for sure.

"You get on your horse and ride out," Tim said. "And be quick about it."

His friend said, "We should finish him off."

"Then you do it, Mike. Go on—you take Fargo on yourself."

But when it came to one on one, Mike was no more eager for a fight than Tim was. "You boys want to help here?"

They were suddenly bashful. They'd been speaking up loud and clear when they thought Tim and Mike were going to do their fighting for them. But now things were different. They muttered, they mumbled, they looked away, they looked down at the ground—they didn't want any part of it.

"Pretty tough group of fellas," Fargo said. "Davis must be real proud of you."

Keeping his gun pointed at Tim, Fargo backed up to his stallion and then mounted up.

"If any of you has any information about where your boss was the other night, there's some money in it for you. But it has to be honest information. There's too much lying going on around this town already."

Tim spoke up. "How much money are we talking about here?"

"Enough to make it worthwhile."

"You ain't telling him nothing," Mike said, shoving Tim. "The boss treats us pretty damned good. You ain't helping this here gunny and I'll see to that, I promise you."

"It's up to you," Fargo said. "You boys like to drink at the Trail's End. I'll be there tonight from nine to ten. If you got anything to tell me, you know where to find me now."

With that, Fargo turned his stallion around and headed back to town. He'd planted a seed he was sure would grow. Glen Davis was a hothead. Being thrown over by Bonnie McLure had to have undone him. Love and money were the reasons for most murders. Davis could claim the first one to a painful degree. But did that mean he was a murderer?

"I always get sad at sundown."

"That could be a song title."

Simone Callahan laughed. "You always have a smart remark, don't you?"

But Fargo wasn't up for verbal fencing. "I try not to think of things like that."

"You don't like to look into yourself? See what's there?"

"Maybe I'm afraid to see what's there. I've had to be pretty violent sometimes, whether I wanted to or not."

They were in Simone's small two-room "flat," as she liked to call it, a front room with two windows with the shades pulled down, a horsehair couch with matching footstool and a deep blue armchair with another matching footstool. A blue area rug was spread across the hardwood floor. The walls held six framed photographs of Simone with people who resembled her in various ways—family.

Fargo was resting on the couch, boots off, his legs stretched out on the horsehair footstool. Outside you could hear wagons and surreys clopping by in the darkness.

"Ready?" Simone said. A small mahogany table next to the kitchen area in the other room was filled with four bottles of alcohol—wine, rye whiskey, bourbon and scotch.

"You're going to get drunk, lady."

"I've got a surprise for you. I'm well on my way. I'm not much of a drinker. All these bottles are courtesy of the bank. The Fourth of July party we had. Theo said I could take them home. I save them for special occasions like this one." She giggled, an actual giggle. "I guess that's why I dressed up, huh?"

She wore a man's shirt and a sloppy pair of butternuts. But nothing could diminish the lacerating sexuality of her aura or the lovely curves of her body. The red hair she wore upswept now had started to come apart in strands that gave her an odd appeal.

"How about half a shot of bourbon, I guess," Fargo said. "I've got a lot to do yet. I can't afford to be drunk."

She brought her drink, wine, and his drink over to him on the couch and then sat down next to him.

Fargo put his head back, closed his eyes. A rest was nice given all the things he had to do tonight. If he was to help Helen Mason, he had to do it fast before all the other forces at work managed to convict Theo once and for all. Fargo just wished he liked some of these people better. This was one of those towns where you divided people by worse, worser and worsest. Not a place he'd want to settle down—if he ever decided that that fateful day had come at last.

He had just dozed off when he felt the soft, tender, warm mouth of Simone Callahan on his, her hands rubbing up and down his chest with great expertise, her luscious breasts pressing against his left arm and causing his manhood to suddenly stand erect.

He managed to set his shot glass on the footstool before she pulled him away from the back of the couch and straightened him so that they could begin to kiss in earnest. He didn't waste time, either. As soon as they were wrapped up in each other, sharing arms and legs, he unbuttoned her shirt and began teasing her nipples with his thumb and forefinger. She erupted—that was the only way to say it. She began frantically helping him strip her nude, both of them tossing her clothes into the air with furious energy.

And then they rolled off the couch so that he was sitting upright and she was mounting herself on his shaft with an almost terrifying soaking passion as he did little more than grab her hips and help her take advantage of his huge hard manhood.

Neither of them had any sense of how long she went on sitting astride him like that but somewhere along the way he slipped out of her and pushed her back up on the couch so he could kneel down and give her the ultimate thrill for women, the deft tongue she had been waiting for.

It didn't take long before her screams bounced off the walls and Fargo remembered that the landlady was hard of hearing. She must be or Simone would have been kicked out long ago.

And when she finished, soaking with sweat and other beautiful fluids, he crawled up on the couch and entered her with a ferocity that matched her own. He varied his strokes, working her up to the top of her passion again, and then he reached under her and took her wet buttocks in his hands and shared his explosive pleasure with her, while she used certain muscles to keep him longer and tighter inside. And then, spent, they both relaxed on different ends of the couch.

"You as good with a gun as you are with women?"

Fargo, rolling a smoke, said, "That's a nice thing to say and I appreciate it. But you're damned good yourself."

"Well, thank you, kind sir. I'm just glad the old lady is deaf."

"I was thinking that myself."

She reached down and snatched her shirt from the

floor, shrugging into it and standing up. "I'm going to have a slice of cheese and some bread with butter. That sound good?"

"I need to get going. But that sounds too good to miss."

While she fixed the food, Fargo got into his clothes. When he was tugging on his boots, he noticed a framed photograph on a small table draped in an enormous white doily. The photograph showed Theo Mason, David McLure and Simone sitting together on bleachers at a baseball game. He held it up and showed it to her.

"McLure and Mason are friends?"

"Used to be best of friends. But not anymore. That, by the way, was the annual baseball game we play against another bank. That was a couple of years back."

"What happened to the friendship?" Fargo said, setting the photograph down on the table again.

She carried two plates over. The slices of cheese were generous. So was the slathered butter on the bread. They both sat on the couch, eating, even though there was a dining table in the west corner.

"I'm not sure," she said. "They're still on speaking terms. And David McLure still does his banking with us. But something happened one night—" She shook her head. "I guess Theo's personal lawyer came over right after the bank closed and the three of them were there until after midnight. The woman who cleans up at night told me that they were shouting at each other—David and Theo, anyway—and that at one point she thought there was an actual physical fight between the two of them that the lawyer had to break up. She said she was afraid that they might start shooting or something."

"But you never found out what it was that made them so mad at each other?"

"No."

"Maybe I should talk to the lawyer."

"That'd be hard to do, Skye. He's been dead for almost a year. Heart attack."

"You can't even guess what got them so stirred up with each other?"

"Afraid I can't. Theo usually lets me know about major developments. He even asks my opinions a lot of the time. But he never gave me a hint about this. We were both working late one night and Theo was drinking and I brought the subject up—but he snapped at me. Said it was none of my business what'd happened between him and David. Said he'd fire me if I ever brought the subject up again. I'd never seen him that angry before. He likes to be slick and in control of things even when he's drinking. But he got so mad, he knocked over his glass when he started shouting at me. Then he picked up his drink and threw it against the wall. Whatever happened between them made him really mad."

Fargo laid his knife and fork on his empty plate. "That was just what I needed, Simone. I appreciate the meal."

Her eyes sparkled even though her near-drunkenness seemed to have faded with their time on the couch and floor. "I hope you appreciate more than just the food."

He smiled. "I don't think I need to answer that. Couldn't you tell?"

She reached across the couch and took his hand. "I'm afraid I'm old-fashioned sometimes. I just wish you weren't drifting through town here."

"Maybe I'll drift back through sometime."

She withdrew her hand. "Now you know that's a lie." And then giggled again.

"I like that little-girl sound."

"The giggle?"

"Yeah."

"Men seem to like that almost as much as they like my breasts."

"I don't think I'd go *that* far."

She giggled again.

Fargo pushed up from the couch. Angled his holster so that it was just where it belonged. And then went over to the chair to pick up his hat.

At the door, she slid her arms around his middle and proceeded to bring almost as much passion to the good-bye as she had to their lovemaking. Fargo didn't object. His own breath started coming faster, too, his heart hammering, his crotch getting smaller with the swelling of his shaft.

"I'm trying to kidnap you, Skye."

"And you're doing a damned good job of it." He pushed gently away. "But I've still got a lot of things to do, Simone."

"When you're done, you could always come back and stay here for the night."

"Don't know what's ahead. I doubt I'll be done for quite a while."

"Well, I can always dream, can't I?"

She slid her arms around him again.

"I gotta get out of here," Fargo laughed, "before you really do kidnap me."

Nothing was colder and darker than a mountain night. Fargo huddled into his sheepskin and lowered his hat to keep the wind off his face as he made his way to the Jayce Cunningham mansion, a Southern Gothic pile of wood and stone that sprawled over the entire top of a wide hill.

Fargo knew, from other investigations he'd been part of, that the most cooperative person was the person who had the most reason to despise the man you wanted information about. In this case, Fargo was seeking out the Negroes who most likely worked in the horse barn where they toiled as blacksmiths and informal veterinarians. Emancipation may have made them free technically but their lot had yet to be improved substantially. Fargo had seen a lot of black faces working for rich white families here.

He knew he was risking his life. TRESPASSERS WILL BE KILLED signs were posted everywhere. Fargo ground-tied the big Ovaro stallion and made his way along the eastern fence where the barns and bunkhouse lay. The cowboys in the bunkhouse were laughing and talking, which was good. They probably wouldn't be on guard for an intruder.

Fargo jumped the fence when he reached the back of the barn. He landed solidly and rushed into the darkness of the two-story home of the horses the operation owned.

Smells of hay, horse piss, horse shit greeted him first. But as he worked his way through the gloom to the front of the place, the smell of fire and hot coals and hot steel came to him. And then the clank of iron on iron, the blacksmith likely fashioning a horseshoe.

Fargo stayed in the shadows, watching the elderly black man do his work. He was as spry as a much younger man despite his somewhat hunched body and his steel gray hair. He pounded away with the care of a true artist. But his tools weren't brush and palette; his tools were hammer, anvil, forge, vise and tongs. And too many people made the mistake of thinking that blacksmithing was a mindless job anybody could do, when in fact blacksmithing required the skill to design, lay out, cut, drill, finish, temper, weld, braze and create other tools for yourself. These were the subtler parts of the task that few ever saw.

The old man stopped to wipe sweat from his forehead. Even though the night was downright cold, this kind of work made for sweaty labor. All the old man wore was a white cotton shirt and a pair of plain gray work pants. No vest, no jacket.

Fargo said, "I'd like to talk to you for a couple of minutes."

He didn't act scared, the old man. He just acted curious. He put the hammer down and turned to Fargo and said, "You're a fool to be walkin' around here. Can't you read the signs?"

"Yeah. But I have to take that chance."

The old man's dark face broke into a bleak smile. "No 'chance' about it, mister. They catch you, they kill you. No questions asked. They throw your body in a buckboard and take you to the funeral home in town. And the marshal—old Harvey—he'll write down trespassing and the file'll be closed on you. Then if you ain't been claimed in twenty-four hours they throw you in a pauper's grave. It's about two feet deep and they leave the soil real loose so the animals can get at you easy-like. You don't want to see them corpses once the animals work 'em over, lemme tell you."

"You live on the ranch here?"

"Little shack of my own behind the trees to the north. Except for the winters, it's all right."

"You see people come and go?"

"If I'm watchin' for somebody, I do. Otherwise, no."
He shook his gray head. "Mister, I can tell you're gonna
ask me something that could get both of us in real deep
trouble. Remember what I told you about the animals
eatin' on them corpses?"

"I just want you to remember last night."

The old man used his tongs to stir the searing-hot
coals. "Now last night, I had a good reason to remember. That was my birthday. At least that's what my
mother said was my birthday. She took to forgettin'
things as I grew up. But that was the date we settled
on anyway."

"You stay on the ranch?"

" 'Course I did. Where else would I go?"

"You stay in your cabin?"

"Yep."

"Any visitors?"

"Just Mr. Cunningham."

"Senior?"

" 'Course, Senior. That boy of his scares me. I walk
wide of him."

"What did Cunningham want?"

"He give me some money for my birthday. He gives
all the hands money on their birthdays. He's got all the
dates writ down on this tablet he keeps in his office."

"How long did he stay?"

"Oh, maybe three, four minutes. He treats us right
but we don't expect him to socialize with us."

"You happen to notice where he went?"

The frown obscured the old man's features. In the red
glow of the coals, his face became a dark, unhappy mask.
"I figgered that's what you'd get around to."

"Why'd you figure that?"

"Because Mr. Cunningham, he told every hand on the
ranch that if anybody was to ask about last night, that
we weren't to say nothing. So I just figgered a stranger
like you kinda sneakin' up on me and all—well, I just
remembered what Mr. Cunningham said."

"Did he go get his horse?"

"I can't say."

"And then he rode off?"

"I can't say that, either."

Fargo sighed. "There's a man sitting in jail. Somebody wants everybody else to think he's guilty."

"That be Mr. Mason?"

"That's right."

"Don't have much time for him. He's a little too friendly with the ladies, especially the married ones. I had me a wife once and she was the same way, only with men. One day I caught her and it was the sorriest day of my life. I thought I was gonna have me a heart attack and die right on the spot. But what I did was just pack all my clothes in a carpetbag and set out on foot. Rode the rails once I got to St. Louie. And I ain't looked back since."

"I'm not saying he's a saint. I don't care for him all that much, myself. But I don't think he's a killer, either. I just need help in figuring out where certain people were last night."

"Cain't help you, mister. Like I said."

"So after he gave you your money, he got on his horse and rode somewhere off the ranch."

The old man smiled again. "Got to admire your persistence, mister." He paused. "I ain't sayin' he didn't ride off and I ain't sayin' he did." The brown eyes turned sly, almost whimsical. "But I can guess what you're thinking and I'd have to say you just might be right."

"So he did ride off?"

"That'd be up to you, mister."

Now Fargo smiled. The old man was a pretty crafty character. "And I don't suppose you noticed when he got back?"

The old man stirred the coals again. A stream of gray smoke rose up. "About eleven every night, I take me my good-night piss. There's a little latrine over there I dug for myself. Anyway, eleven's when I usually go out there and it wasn't no different last night. And I seen a horse and rider comin' back to the ranch here, ridin' fast right up to the house."

"And that was Jayce Cunningham?"

The old man laughed, enjoying himself. "I ain't sayin' it was and I ain't sayin' it wasn't. But I can guess what you're thinking and I'd have to say you just might be right."

Fargo patted the old man on his shoulder. "I'd hate to see you on a witness stand. You'd have everybody confused."

"I learned a long time ago to say things in a round-about way. You live longer."

"I appreciate it."

Just then the voices of two men drifted toward them. Heavy boot steps. Coming in this direction.

"I was you, I'd skedaddle right now, mister. There're a lot more of them than there is of you."

"Thanks. I appreciate your help."

And with that, Fargo hurried out of the barn and back to his stallion.

There were saloons and there were saloons. Some of them tried to impress you with a clean environment devoid of puking-fighting-shooting gents. There were free hard-boiled eggs for the customers and a player piano man who could tinkle out just about any song you wanted to hear. And the whores were clean, which the bartender hurried to tell you. Fargo had known a few places where the bartender would show you a recent letter from a local doc testifying that he'd examined these girls himself and found them to be clean. He'd even sign his name to it, putting his reputation on the line.

And then there were saloons. These were where you *did* find the pukers-fighters-shooters. Fortunately, Fargo seemed to have hit the Trail's End when these types of fellas were home resting.

The place was nothing fancy but it was clean. There were three card games going, each player looking to be older than sixty and eager to keep everything friendly. These men probably all went to the same church together. They played for fun, not blood.

The bartender was a tired little man about Fargo's age. "Closin' up in an hour."

"Hope my business'll be done by then."

The bartender's trim mustache twitched nervously. "You mind if I ask what kind of business?"

"Afraid I gotta keep that to myself. But it's nothing that will give you any problems, I can promise you that. Meanwhile why don't you push a beer my way?"

When Fargo got his beer, he carried it over to an empty table and began his wait.

In the meantime, he went over all the points of the two murders. They certainly didn't want for suspects. Damned near everybody he'd met had revealed himself to have a motive. What eluded him so far was the connection between the two killings.

He kept a close eye on the batwings. They were pushed open six times in the first forty-five minutes of his wait. The problem was that none of them were the ranch hands he'd hoped to see here.

His third time back at the bar for more beer, the little man said, "Twenty minutes—that's five extra minutes so them boys over there can finish up their card game—I gotta shut the doors. The owner's a real fussbudget about closing time." He shoved a beer at Fargo. "I take it your 'business' didn't work out." He yawned. "Anyways, I'm tired. The wife and me took a vacation down the river. Real nice place and on the cheap side, too. Only thing that spoiled it was David McLure pushin' people around. He's a nasty one when he drinks. Spoiled the whole trip back for us. Lotta people on the boat wanted to throw him overboard." He smiled at the last line. "My wife's birthday's the seventeenth. That was the second day on the trip back. Ruined the whole day for her. Never seen a man make an entire steamship mad before. It was a little one—the ship, I mean—but it was still a lot of people."

Fargo had positioned himself on one elbow at the bar so that he was partially facing the batwings.

Finally, the man behind the bar picked up a miniature Chinese gong and banged on it several times. The sound was surprisingly loud.

"All right, men. You've got three minutes to fold up. Sorry to do this to you but them's the orders I got."

The card players grumbled; the solitary drinkers threw back their beers and whiskey. A few of the solitary ones looked damned mad about having to journey out into the cold, dark night again.

"You, too, mister."

Fargo nodded. Loyalty or fear had kept the ranch

hands from coming here and sharing what they knew with Fargo. He'd been stupid to think they'd show up.

He tossed some coins on the bar and said, "Put that toward your next vacation."

"I just hope David McLure don't show up while me and the missus are enjoying ourselves."

Fargo said, "You're sure right about that. I could live a long time without ever seeing him again."

"Somebody left this letter for you, Mr. Fargo."

Fargo walked over to the desk. The night clerk, a man who wore sleeve garters and a sleek thin mustache, pushed a white envelope toward him. The envelope said: FARGO. Nothing else.

"You happen to see who left this for me?"

"Afraid I didn't, Mr. Fargo. I just came on about half an hour ago. I can go ask Andy, the day man today. He's in the taproom."

"I'd appreciate it if you'd do that."

The clerk came out from around the desk and crossed the floor to the hallway that would take him to the taproom. Meanwhile, Fargo stared at the envelope. He wasn't sure why but he felt that this could be a trap of some kind. He'd been misled before, usually as a way of luring him into a dangerous situation. Of course, if anybody wanted to kill him, they wouldn't have a hard time finding him. He wasn't exactly hiding. But there was always the chance that in the open somebody would see who the shooter was. But what if somebody lured Fargo with the promise of information to a dark site where nobody would see him being killed? Obviously, the killer of Bonnie McLure and—he was sure—the killer of old man McLure was starting to close in on Fargo. He couldn't let the Trailsman nose around much longer without finding out something that would clear Theo Mason.

The clerk came back trailed by the day man, a short, curly-haired, middle-aged gent with a broken nose and the general air of a tough guy.

"You Fargo?"

"That's me."

"I'm Andy Hannity. I'm the substitute day man. Other

man was sick today. Usually I work in the office and do the books. Bob here tells me you want to know about the letter." *Shows you can't judge a book by its cover,* Fargo thought. To look at Andy Hannity, you'd think of a brawler. But his voice and words were sociable, even amiable, and his manner friendly and cooperative.

"I'd appreciate that, yes."

"Well, I wish I could help you but I can't."

"Oh? Why's that?"

"Pretty simple. I was behind the desk here—we were pretty busy this morning—and somebody yelled there was a fire in one of the wooden boxes we keep right outside the back door for trash. I hated to leave because I was the only one here but since the lobby was empty I figured I'd be all right for a minute or two. Plus we don't take any chances with fires, not even the smallest kind. So I rushed back there and got a bucket of water and a bucket of sand and put it out."

Fargo was way ahead of him. Sometimes the old tricks worked best of all. Create a diversion, get the desk clerk to leave his post, and then leave the letter when nobody was watching.

"So the letter was on the desk when you got back?"

"Sitting out in plain sight."

"Anybody in the lobby?"

"No, it was still empty."

"Well, thanks. I appreciate you coming here and telling me in person."

Andy Hannity grinned. "You did me a favor. The wife told me she wants me home exactly one half hour after my shift is over. I've already overstayed. You helped get me out of the taproom." He nodded to the letter in Fargo's hand. "Again, sorry I couldn't be any help."

Upstairs in his room, Fargo finally opened the letter.

The iron horse statue by the river in the park. Tonight at 11:00. I have information that could get me killed.

Unsigned, of course.

The handwriting obviously belonged to a woman, a

careful kind of penmanship rendered in blue ink. The paper was white, unlined, unremarkable.

A trap.

That was still Fargo's first response to the letter. But, the more he thought about it, the more he realized that a trap could be turned to his advantage. It was one way to find out who the real killer was.

As far as he was concerned, Jayce Cunningham, Glen Davis and David McLure were all still suspects in Bonnie McLure's murder. Maybe one of them had sent this letter. Maybe one of them would be waiting there to kill him.

He spent a few minutes checking his Colt. He enjoyed working with guns, the smell of the oil, the ease with which the gun parts moved, the gleam of the barrel in the lamplight and the hefty feeling of the checkered grips when the gun was back in its holster.

The night had flipped a page on the calendar. It now felt like November, bitter lancing winds, ice forming on small puddles that gleamed in the moonlight, breath emerging from mouths in frosty plumes.

He was almost half an hour early but that was all right. He wanted to scope out the entire park landscape so he could see who had come to meet him. He wanted the advantage of surprising his visitor.

He just hadn't planned on how damned cold it was.

Beth Farrell had always wanted to tell Mrs. McLure about what David had forced her to do those six or seven times over the spring of the year before. But Beth knew that even if she believed it, Mrs. McLure would deny it because she was one of those women who wanted peace at any cost in her home. The other maid had whispered to Beth that such a thing had happened before and all Mrs. McLure had done was fire the girl and sternly warn the others not to be making up lies about her husband.

But Beth knew they were getting rid of her. A new girl had appeared yesterday. Mrs. McLure showed her off the way she would a new surrey or a new dress. She gave the young woman a tour of the place, introduced her to the children and even invited her to dinner so that everybody could meet her in a relaxed setting.

The other maid told Beth that this meant that either she or Beth would be fired soon. And Beth knew instantly which of them it would be.

Her biggest problem was that she always sent half her earnings home to her mother, who had taken suddenly sick after the death of Beth's father. The only one left to support her was Beth's lazy brother, who was never able to hold a job for more than two or three weeks at a time. He always whined that the people were "too stupid to work with." Could that possibly be because he was a know-it-all who couldn't resist telling the owner of a place everything he was doing wrong? And then telling the owner what he, Ambrose William Farrell, recommended as a way to "save" the business?

She'd have to find another job quickly. Her mother needed help for her heart problems.

But tonight—and this was even better than money— Beth Farrell was going to get satisfaction. Revenge. She'd sent a note to the man named Fargo. The man who was trying to find out who really killed Bonnie McLure. And old man McLure.

She'd written everything down carefully and hidden it in the folds of her dark Sunday-best dress. She wanted a precise record of her facts. She would tell Fargo everything she knew. But the long letter would give him something to refer to when he went after the real culprit.

She wished now that she'd worn more than a shawl. She'd hitched a ride with one of the cowboys driving a buckboard into town. He'd be coming back to the ranch at midnight after the card game at the lodge. He showed her where he would leave the buckboard. If she was there at midnight, he'd give her a ride back.

Now she approached the park. And realized that somebody was following her. Or was pretty sure somebody was following her. She'd had this same impression on the way into town. She couldn't explain it—when she turned around she never saw anybody—but it was just there, this feeling.

But she wouldn't let it stop her.

Bowing her head to push through a brutal headwind,

wrapping the shawl around her ever tighter, she made her way to the park, stepping carefully because of the gleaming patches of ice. All she needed was a broken leg. Who'd hire somebody with a broken leg?

The wind pushed back against her, a young woman who weighed not quite a hundred pounds, frail in such a blast, almost knocked over at one point. The night had taken on sinister aspects by now, the stores all dark, the street empty, the wind rattling windows and the shadows seeming to hide unimaginable threats.

She put her head even lower and plodded forward, trying to anchor herself with heavy, deliberate steps. But the ferocity of the wind still overpowered her, so much so that she was unaware of the figure coming up from behind her, a figure in a dark duster with a low-brimmed black hat pulled down so far that seeing a face was impossible.

A straight knife, unadorned, the kind you could buy three for a dollar from a Sears catalog or two for a dollar at the local hardware store—a straight knife glinted in the right gloved hand as the figure caught up with her quickly.

Turned her around with great sudden violence that did what the wind hadn't been able to do—knock her to the ground with such force that she smashed the back of her head on the frozen rut of a wagon track that had been simple mud earlier in the day.

Making the figure's work much, much easier.

Fargo could claim several virtues. Unfortunately, patience wasn't included among any of them.

His visitor was fifteen minutes late. He leaned against a tree, trying to get a smoke going in the wind. For the first time he considered the possibility that the letter was a ruse. Somebody toying with him, wasting his time, trying to confuse him. Harvey would do something like this. Or a townsperson who simply didn't like the idea of an outsider messing in the town's business.

The river's tissue of ice gleamed silver in the moonlight. The rowboats run up on shore on the other side looked lonely, discards from the hot months when they'd borne lovers and families up and down the river for various festivities. He shuddered inside his sheepskin. He could use a few hot months right now himself.

And then he saw near the bridge to the west the sight of torches flickering in the night. A crowd of some kind. He was too far away to hear anything that was being said. But he sensed that the crowd somehow had something to do with the failure of the letter writer to show up. The only thing that would bring a torch-lit crowd out on a night like this was violence. People always came out for violence. It topped coming out for money or sex. Give 'em a little blood and they'd show up for sure.

He flicked his cigarette into the darkness and started for the long path that eventually led to the street and the bridge. The closer he got, the larger the crowd got. Women in winter bonnets and heavy coats joined men in winter dusters and sheepskins looking down at something that Fargo couldn't yet see.

And then he saw Harvey standing next to David McLure, David shaking his head as if in profound grief. Harvey saw Fargo before McLure did. He smirked and waved him over.

Fargo walked around the outside of the crowd that smelled of sleep, tobacco, liquor. The shock of it had worn off for some of them already. They'd gotten the drug kick they'd wanted—was any drug as powerful as the sight of death, the same death they'd be dying someday?—and were now beginning to drift away.

Then McLure saw him. He didn't smirk. He frowned and leaned in and whispered something to Harvey. Harvey smiled, as if relishing a secret told on Fargo.

"I take it somebody's dead," Fargo said.

"You're a real mastermind, Fargo," Harvey said.

"At least I'm not bought and paid for."

Fargo's remark stung Harvey. He grimaced and actually looked embarrassed.

"You've had your fun. I want you gone from here by sunup. And if you think I'm bluffing, try me. I could figure out about twenty different town ordinances you've violated, Fargo. And that means runnin' you over to county jail for six to nine months. And them boys ain't kind and understanding like ole Harve, believe me."

Fargo said, "Maybe it'd help if you two would tell me what the hell's going on here."

"Beth," McLure said. "Beth Farrell."

Only now did Fargo know who McLure was talking about. The young day maid at the McLure mansion—Beth Farrell.

"Somebody killed Beth Farrell?"

"Don't bother putting on a show for us," McLure said. "You know who was killed here tonight."

"Somebody cut her throat real good. Real good, Fargo, let me tell you." Harvey sounded truly sickened by what he'd seen.

"I don't suppose anybody saw anything? You've been looking for witnesses by now?" Fargo knew he was taking another jab at Harvey's incompetence but at the moment he didn't give a damn. He'd been fond of Beth. She hadn't belonged in such a hothouse of greed and gloom as the McLure mansion.

"You have your methods and I have mine," Harvey said. "And if you don't want to spend a good long time in jail, I'd advise you to keep your mouth shut and to be gone by sunup. You're the first person I'll check on in the morning and you'd damned well better be gone."

A wagon clattered up. A stern voice said, "Let me through. I need to pick up the body." The mortician, Ambrose Harte, was making a lot of money these days. The lanky man with the top hat and dramatic cape didn't seem to mind the wind at all. What was a little wind when the charge to the town was guaranteed? Didn't have to go chasing after any welshers when the money came in a draft from the town bookkeeper.

And then once again the other two on Fargo's suspect list arrived separately and within two minutes of each other. Jayce Cunningham strolled over with the air of a man overseeing his own property—the whole town. He watched as Ambrose Harte and his assistant got the body up to the wagon and shoved it into the bed of the vehicle. People made room for him, of course. Wherever he went, people stood back making room. Fear more than any respect played in their eyes.

Neither fear nor respect showed in those same eyes

135

when Glen Davis appeared. He had to fight his way through the crowd. Both men made their way to Fargo and the others.

"This town is going to hell, Harvey," Jayce said in his godlike voice. "This murder rate is ridiculous for a town this size. We want to attract people here, not scare them off."

Harvey resented being chastened in front of others this way. You could speak to him privately and call him any name you wanted. He was used to it. His entire career had been as the lackey of men more powerful than himself. But the unwritten rule with Harvey was "Say it in private."

"And I see Mr. Fargo's still with us, too. I don't like Mr. Fargo smelling up our town even worse. I asked you to get rid of him and you haven't done that, either."

"He'll be gone by dawn, Jayce."

"That something he said or something you said?"

"Something I didn't just 'say,' Jayce. Something I warned him about."

"That's what I'm talking about, Harvey," Jayce said. His voice was gentler now. "He hasn't done one damned thing you've told him to since he got here. Why should he take you seriously anymore?"

"Because he'll go to jail for a good long time if he don't."

Jayce shook his head. "I hope you're right, Harvey. For the sake of the town and for the sake of your job."

Fargo said, "Harvey, here's something to think about. Neither Jayce nor Glen Davis here has a good alibi for the night Bonnie McLure died. Why don't you ask them where they were?"

"You're accusing Jayce Cunningham of bein' a murderer?" Harvey sounded as outraged as Jayce would have himself.

"I'm saying it's a possibility."

"Put him in jail right now, Harvey," Jayce said. "And that's an order."

No more mask, no more disguise. Jayce Cunningham was making it very clear who actually ran the law in this town. And it wasn't town marshal Harvey DeLong, that was for damned sure. If he hadn't been humiliated by

Jayce's earlier bullying, Harvey might've meekly complied with Jayce's demand. But even whores have pride and Harvey wanted to demonstrate this by not giving in to it. "I gave him till dawn, Jayce. If he isn't gone by then, you can visit him in the jailhouse. How's that?"

"I guess you didn't hear me right, Harvey. I said I wanted him thrown in jail now. Not tomorrow morning. And I don't give a damn what you told him. I want him in custody right now."

"That's kind of funny, Cunningham," Fargo said. "I was under the impression that Harvey was the town marshal. Must be you who really wears the badge, huh?"

"I don't like this man, Harvey," Cunningham said. "And I don't know how I can make it any plainer to you."

"He said sunup and that still stands until Harvey tells me otherwise. Now if he wants to shoot me in the back, that's fine. But otherwise I'm going to walk away right now."

"You're not going to let him do that, are you?" McLure growled. "Harvey, you heard what Jayce said. Now arrest this punk."

"I'm walking away, Harvey. It's your call now."

"Harvey—" Jayce snapped. "Do your job!"

But Fargo had glimpsed Harvey's expression. The old man had been humiliated in front of the townspeople. And the humiliation made it clear to everybody what had long been rumored—that he was nothing but the bought and paid for lawman for the rich and powerful. A puppet, at best. And something in him resisted this latest order. He'd spoken his mind when he'd given Fargo till sunup to get out of town. And he wasn't going to change his mind just because Jayce Cunningham told him to.

Harvey said, "You got till sunup, Fargo."

Fargo nodded and turned around, walking toward the ragged remnants of the crowd. He didn't get far.

"Well, if you won't do it, I will!" McLure bellowed and caught up to Fargo in four long rushing strides.

But Fargo had expected resistance. And was ready for it. As soon as McLure's hand grabbed Fargo's shoulder, the Trailsman spun around and slammed a right-handed uppercut into the other man's jaw. He followed this up immediately with a smashing left hand to the temple and then sailed an easy punch straight to the Adam's apple. McLure was in so much pain and confusion, he literally didn't know how to fall down. He leaned left, he leaned right, he seemed about to go over backward—and then he simply collapsed into a pile.

Jayce said, "Damn you, Harvey, arrest this man now or you're finished in this town. You understand me?"

Then Harvey did a funny thing. "You gonna help me here, Fargo, and let me lock you up for a while? I'm too old to find another job."

"Well, if this isn't the most disgusting spectacle I've ever seen—" Cunningham blustered.

But Fargo thought it was mostly funny. The old man was begging for his job. Fargo saw an opportunity here. He knew that as much as he hated Harvey, he now needed to pretend he felt friendly toward him. Harvey could be a help. So Fargo had to choke down memories of the beating the marshal had given him, memories of all the men Harvey had taken into his little room—and pretend to cooperate with the lawman.

"I get a lawyer?"

"I'll see to it personally," Harvey said.

Fargo shrugged. "You make pretty good coffee. I guess I've spent a night in worse places." He walked back to the lawman and said, "Put the cuffs on me, Harvey."

"I didn't think you could disgrace your office any more than you already have, Harvey," Cunningham said, "but this is the lowest you've sunk yet."

As he was putting the cuffs on Fargo, Harvey said, "You said arrest. I've arrested. You said put him in jail. And I'm about to do that. I don't know what you're complaining about, Jayce." He said this in a droll way that had the citizens snickering. It was fun to see a powerful man like Jayce slapped around like this.

One of the deputies was now helping McLure to his feet. The man still seemed dazed, not sure what had happened or where he was. He muttered nonsense. "Maybe I should take him to the doc's."

"The doc's gonna be pretty drunk this time of night,"

Jayce said, "get the doc's wife to tend to him. She's better than the doc anyway."

"Well, he's the one with the degree, sir," the deputy said politely.

"Yeah, from a college nobody can find a record of anyplace," Jayce shot back. "Now do what I tell you."

Afraid now, the deputy said, "Yessir."

Jayce Cunningham stepped over to Fargo. "Once you're in that cell, that's your home for a good long time and I can guarantee that. And the next man we hire as marshal won't be as friendly as Harvey here." He glared at Harvey. "Maybe you can get a job swabbing out saloons, Harvey. That's about all you're good for anymore." And with that, he charged through the crowd that parted like the Red Sea for this imposing and angry man.

Harvey smiled. "Figgered it'd come to this someday. Kind of inevitable, I guess. Only so much ass a man can kiss."

He led Fargo away, across the bridge to town. Only a few in the crowd followed. The deputies went on ahead in case a crowd formed there. Harvey told them to send people home before they had a chance to form a mob that would be a nuisance more than anything. They didn't have anybody to support in this situation. They didn't like Harvey, Jayce or Fargo. They just wanted to see somebody get debased or hurt—preferably both.

"You got me in a lot of trouble out there," Harvey said, once they were inside the marshal's office.

"You got yourself in trouble. They kept goading you and you went along with it. Jayce had to prove to everybody that you were his little dancing dog. Wasn't anything I could do."

Harvey led Fargo to the back of the place. Theo Mason watched him being led to a cell of his own. Harvey said, "I already let Seth Parker go."

A mouse raced through the bars of one cell and into the other. "I'll take the one without the mouse," Fargo said.

"Picky sumbitch for a drifter." And then he smiled at Fargo. "I don't much like 'em either."

Fargo went into the cell.

"Hands over your head."

The search yielded Fargo's gun, knife and money, all of which the lawman made quick work of.

"You just get settled in and I'll be back here in about half an hour."

"We're supposed to talk, remember?"

"Oh, I remember, all right. Nothing I'd like more than to figure out that Jayce was involved in these murders."

"You'd really go after him?"

"What do I have to lose? He's gonna throw me out of town in a day or two anyway. Even if I can just plant a seed of doubt, that'll be good enough for me. He's always lived so high-and-mighty—see how he likes everybody watchin' him all the time, thinking he's guilty. He won't like it at all, believe me."

Fargo surprised himself by drifting off into a light sleep almost immediately. When he woke up he wasn't sure where he was. All he knew for sure was that he was in trouble. Jail bars sort of send that message loud and clear.

But as he swung his legs off the cot and started the process of rolling a smoke, the rest of it came back all too clearly—all too clearly indeed. He looked over at Theo Mason and said, "I was hoping I'd never have to see your ugly face again, especially not in a place like this."

Despite all his troubles, Theo actually laughed. "I could say the same thing about you, you bastard. But I'd rather see you than Jayce Cunningham. He came here and called me names even I had never heard of. I think I'd rather face a lynch mob than face him again."

But Fargo didn't even smile. "That's not anything to joke about."

Never steal keepsakes, Ambrose Harte had decided long ago. Keepsakes, they'd come after you. The watch somebody had given the deceased for an important anniversary or the gold ring for the wedding or the pinkie ring from the boss. These were the sort of things the loved ones remembered, and if they weren't on the body when the body was delivered, there'd be hell to pay.

And the first person they'd look to for payment was the man who'd prepared the body for shipping or burial.

Ambrose Harte, despite following exactly the rules set forth in the *Undertaker's Manual*, was always suspected of deviousness by his fellow townspeople.

He was thinking these things as he began preparing the body of the young woman who'd been murdered on the bridge tonight. She lay on the pyre in his back room awaiting embalming with his particular formula—four ounces of arsenious acid per gallon of water to be used as the embalming fluid.

First, he had to deal with the clothes. Females her age and her size—he preferred stout, middle-aged women— offered him no sexual appeal whatsoever. So he made quick and officious work of her. In just a few minutes he had her clothes laid neatly out on a table next to where he worked. He barely noticed that she was naked.

What he did notice, though, was the folded piece of paper that had floated to the floor from her full skirt.

He walked over to it, snatched it up and began reading.

And then he began trembling.

In this town the one thing you didn't want to do was go up against any of the powerful families. This letter— and he couldn't be sure to whom it had been written— wouldn't merely get him run out of town. It might very well get him shot.

He leaned against the wall. His face gleamed with sweat. What to do with it? Who could he take it to? He might as well give it to Harvey. The letter would give the lawman a little power as he was being pushed out of town. He could leave on his own terms.

That was the best way to live, Ambrose Harte, master ass-kisser and toady for all the rich men in town, reasoned . . . on your own terms.

"You're not coming to bed?"

"Can't sleep."

"You still have your coat on."

"None of your damned business what I have on. Now get back to bed."

"Maybe I'm concerned about you."

Jayce Cunningham looked up from the desk in his study. In fact, he'd been so preoccupied with his thoughts that he hadn't realized he was still wearing his coat.

Then he said, "Louisa, I'm sorry. I shouldn't have talked to you like that. You're one of the few people who really worries about me. I apologize."

The elderly maid smiled. "If I took your gibes seriously, Jayce, I would've left here a long time ago. Now why don't you take your coat off and go upstairs and get a good night's sleep? I'll bring you some warm milk if you'd like."

He stared out the black moonless window. "Harvey stood up to me tonight. Disobeyed me and in front of everybody."

"Harvey did? That's pretty hard to imagine."

"It's all because of that damned Fargo. I think Fargo gave old Harvey ideas about acting on his own. Running things as he sees them rather than as I see them. And that's dangerous."

Louisa was Jayce's confessor. He'd long confided all his problems to her. He'd had a wife who'd been fastidiously bored with his business problems. Louisa was older than he was by five years. He'd always wondered if that was why she was, at least in some ways, so much wiser. Others saw nothing but a slight, ancient gray-haired crone in Louisa. Jayce saw something very much like a shaman.

"The worst thing was that Harvey disobeyed me in public. By tomorrow morning it'll be all over town. I give him a direct order and he disobeys me." He was repeating himself but then he often did that when he was upset. Louisa was used to it. She waited him out patiently. "I should go over there right now and take his gun and his badge."

"And that would accomplish what?"

He smiled at her. "The voice of reason. You always question everything I suggest."

"You forget good judgment sometimes with your temper."

He sighed. True. Was that the right thing to do—go

142

charging into the town marshal's office and demand that Harvey hand over badge, gun, keys? By the time the town awoke, Harvey would have been fired. That would make a much better story for the morning—much better anyway than the one that had Harvey publicly disobeying Jayce and at least temporarily getting away with it.

"I think that's what I should do, Louisa." But it wasn't a statement; it was a question. He was really asking her permission.

"You don't have many choices at this time. The important thing is to save face. The important thing is to remind the town that you're in charge, not Harvey and certainly not this Fargo." She paused. "If you were forced to kill Harvey—"

He looked up sharply. "You're serious?"

"Of course. Somebody crosses Jayce Cunningham and he gets killed for his trouble. How would that be? Even David McLure'd have to think about that one. He wouldn't try and overrule you so often."

But Jayce looked dispirited. "I don't— Harvey and me go way back."

"That'd make it all the more effective. Old friends, loyalty going back decades—but you did what you had to when Harvey acted up—acted against the better good of this town. You killed him. They'll be talking about that for years to come, Jayce."

He looked down at his boots. He was all ready to walk out the door. Hadn't taken off a single thing except his hat since coming indoors. He was beginning to see Louisa's point. His reputation had waned somewhat as his birthdays had mounted up. People still feared him but not as they once had. If he was to kill old Harvey—

He stood up, a huge man in his bulky black winter coat with the capelike back. "I'll think about it, Louisa. I'll go over there and see what's going on and I'll think about it."

She came to him and clung to his arm. "If you're smart, Jayce, you'll do it. Show everybody that the old Jayce still exists."

He pushed past her, on his way to the side door. The wind was a siren's cry now.

Louisa stood in the window watching him go, a hulking black figure in the shadowy night. She prayed he would kill Harvey. She no longer got the same respect from the domestics of other homes that she once had. That showed her that Jayce was no longer as feared as he'd once been. But if he were to kill Harvey . . .

"Maybe head down the Mississippi," Harvey said, sipping his coffee. "Always wanted to do that."

"New Orleans?"

"Maybe, Fargo. Or maybe over to Florida. Not so crowded there."

They sat in Harvey's office. As they talked, Fargo was writing out his list of suspects so they could get to work. Funny that Fargo would end up working with a crooked lawman like Harvey, especially one who treated prisoners so violently. But in the West you didn't always have much choice about whom you threw in with, not if you wanted to get the job done.

"Could I get some coffee back here?" Theo Mason called from the cell in back.

Fargo snorted. "My turn or yours?"

"Yours. You're younger."

Fargo pushed himself up from his chair. He made a quick pass by the potbelly stove where the coffeepot sat, poured a cup and then carried it back to the cell block. Three of the cells were occupied.

Only Theo was awake. He stood with his hand through the cell bars, waiting impatiently. He took the cup, carefully working it through the bars. For the sake of those asleep—apparently forgetting that he'd bellowed out his request—he whispered, "I sure hope you can get me out of here, Fargo. I'm starting to go crazy."

"I'm doing the best I can." Then he paused. The front door had opened. Somebody had come in. Heavy footsteps made their way down the hall, stopping about where Harvey's office was.

"You probably don't believe this but I'm going to reform—completely. And I mean completely."

"Completely" usually meant about two weeks in Fargo's experience. But he just let it ride. Theo had the right idea if nothing else.

"Drink your coffee," Fargo whispered. He wanted to get back up front, see who'd come in.

He was three steps toward that goal when the two shots cracked through the silence. He started running. Instinct. He had no gun. Harvey had taken it.

Outside Harvey's office stood one of his deputies, a man named Hap Bowers. Hap, looking shocked and sick, leaned against the wall.

"What happened?" Fargo said.

And then through the door stepped Jayce Cunningham, six-shooter still smoking.

"What happened? That's pretty easy, Mr. Fargo. You started nosing around and stirred up a lot of trouble. For some reason, you had poor old Harvey convinced that he was running his own show here and didn't have to listen to anybody. And that's why he drew down on me, I guess."

Fargo glanced at Bowers. "Harvey drew down on Cunningham here?"

Bowers lowered his head.

"Tell 'em, Bowers. Go on. You saw it all."

Bowers could barely raise his head. "I seen it. I seen it all."

"Dammit, Bowers, raise your head and speak up. I want Fargo to hear what you saw."

Bowers' face was now slick with sweat. His head came up slowly. He looked at Fargo. "Harvey, he got mad at Mr. Cunningham and he went for his gun. And Mr. Cunningham, he didn't have any choice. He had to draw. And he killed Harvey."

"Pure self-defense—is that right, Bowers?"

"That's right, sir."

This time, Bowers glanced away, as if he were going to throw up at the lies he'd been telling.

"As for you, Fargo," Jayce Cunningham said, as if addressing a great gathering, "I'm going to surprise you. I'm going to send you packing. I'm going to give you exactly one hour to ride out of this town of ours and never return. Never even pass through."

Fargo wanted to smash the bastard in the face. Maybe Harvey hadn't been much of a man, but he'd been more of a man than this creature. But he knew that his only hope of finding the killer—maybe the killer stood right in front of him, Mr. Jayce Cunningham himself—was to take Cunningham up on his offer.

"And in case you're wondering why I'm letting you ride out, Fargo, it's simple enough. Too many killings. We don't need any more. We're trying to build this community up. Nobody wants to move to a Wild West town. Those days are behind us. Tomorrow I'll be putting the right man into Harvey's job. We'll get this all cleaned up and things'll be back to normal."

At any other time, Fargo would have laughed. He was beginning to suspect what Cunningham was up to here but he couldn't let on.

"There's my Colt on Harvey's desk. I'd like to take it with me."

"Bowers," Cunningham said, "get Fargo his gun. But keep him covered until he's out the front door."

"Yessir."

Bowers went into Harvey's office, retrieved the Colt. He kept his own Colt trained on Fargo the whole time. When he handed Fargo the gun, Fargo thanked him for it.

"Now if you'd be so kind as to escort Mr. Fargo to the front door and then to walk him over to the livery."

"Yessir."

"Can't ask for anything fairer than that, can you, Fargo?"

Fargo shrugged. "Guess not."

The door opened and in came Ambrose Harte, the undertaker. He smelled gunpowder and he smelled blood. He surveyed the faces standing in a semicircle in front of him.

Jayce Cunningham said, "You'll need to get your wagon. Harvey got out of hand and I had to kill him. Pure self-defense, as Bowers here will tell you."

Fargo watched Harte's face carefully. He looked both startled and angry. Cunningham's words hadn't pacified him at all. Then Harte stared at Fargo as if he was trying to send a message of some kind.

Jayce said, "Now let's get this cleared up. Dawn'll be here soon and people'll be stopping by. Harte, you heard me. Get Harvey out of here. And, Bowers, you get

146

Fargo over to the livery and out of town. Now get to it, both of you."

Fargo led the way out. He still wasn't quite sure what he was going to do but he knew he wasn't going to leave town.

A streak of pearl appeared across the bottom of the horizon as the moon began to fade slightly in the dark blue sky. Frost furred everything. Even a block away you could hear the horses in the livery waking, soon to be joined by roosters and dogs.

As Bowers and Fargo walked down the street, footsteps slapped loudly behind them. Ambrose Harte, slightly out of breath, caught up with them. He took some folded papers he carried and jabbed them at Fargo. "You left these behind."

Fargo remembered the strange look that Harte had given him back in the marshal's office. Obviously, whatever these papers were, Harte considered them important. He clearly hadn't been happy about what had happened in the office, this sudden power grab by Jayce Cunningham. So naturally Fargo was curious about the papers he'd just been handed.

Before he could ask any questions, though, the undertaker had turned around and was walking back toward the marshal's office. He obviously didn't want to be around when Fargo looked the papers over.

The livery was coming to life. The stove was boiling coffee, the man on duty was hanging out the OPEN sign and the animals in their stalls were making restless sounds.

Bowers went right to work. Fargo walked back to his stallion. Bowers was right behind him with his saddle. They got the horse ready and Fargo said, "I got time for a cup of coffee?"

Bowers shrugged. "Up to you. But I'd make it a quick one. Jayce has got a hair up his butt. I was surprised he let you go in the first place."

Fargo smiled. "You think I don't know what's going on?"

Bowers' eyes got nervous. "I don't know what you're talking about."

Fargo said, "Sure, you do. You follow me out of town, shoot me in the back and then bury me somewhere."

Fargo slipped his foot in the stirrup and then swung up in the saddle. "Nothing personal, Bowers, but I plan to kill you before you kill me. So I'd just stay here if I were you."

And with that he rode out of the back door of the barn.

Beth wasn't the world's best speller but she sure had a fascinating story to tell.

Fargo sat at a table in a grubby café at the edge of town, reading the letter that began:

Dear Misster Farrago

It went on to detail who had committed the murders of both old man McLure and Bonnie. And now Beth herself.

Fargo had two cups of coffee to fortify himself against what promised to be a cold, bleak day. Then he went out, mounted up and headed for the McLure mansion.

David McLure had recovered pretty well from Fargo's punches. By the time Fargo reached the McLure spread, McLure was getting his buggy ready for town. When he glanced over his shoulder and saw Fargo, the first thing he did was reach inside the rig and grab his carbine.

But Fargo already had his Colt aimed at him. "Make it easy for both of us, McLure."

Fargo had kept his voice down but there was no way his sudden presence had gone unnoticed. Several of the hands, just walking up from the bunkhouse, spotted Fargo instantly and drew their guns.

McLure smiled. "Come in closer, boys. Don't be afraid to shoot Mr. Fargo in the back, either. I believe he's come here to kill me so that gives you all the excuse you need to gun him down."

Fargo said, "Just remember one thing, men. He goes first. You'll get me but I'll get him." He turned in his saddle so that he could see most of them. "And for what it's worth, I don't plan to kill him. I just want him to take a little ride with me. There's no need for any trouble here."

The five men had spread out around Fargo. In truth they could probably get him before he had a chance to kill McLure. But McLure wasn't up for taking any chances.

"Maybe he's right, Tom. You and the boys go about your chores and I'll deal with this."

"You sure, Mr. McLure?"

"Positive. You heard him. He just wants to go for a little ride."

"You sure you trust him?"

"Just get back to work now. And that's my last word."

Whatever arrogance he'd displayed two minutes ago was gone. He knew that Fargo wouldn't need much of an excuse to kill him.

The men started drifting away. They didn't like their boss much but they liked the stranger even less.

"Get in the buggy, McLure. We're headin' into town."

"That's where I was headin' anyway."

"Good. Then I won't be troublin' you any. Right now I want you to drop your Colt and your carbine on the ground. Fast."

McLure hesitated, as if he might try to shoot Fargo. But he quickly backed off. He frowned but did as he was told.

They set off. The horses snorted silvery breath. The buggy jiggled between frozen mud ruts.

Fargo stayed next to the vehicle, his Colt ready.

"I s'pose you've got this whole thing figured out. Or think you do."

"Matter of fact, I have. When you killed your father, you didn't realize that Beth was right outside his study. Seth was a lot drunker than he'll admit to. You didn't have any problem dragging him into your father's study and making him look like the killer. You planted Theo's gun outside so somebody would find it. Harvey would let Seth go and everybody would focus on Theo. The whole thing would look a lot more believable if Seth was charged and then let go. If you'd just planted Theo's gun it might look suspicious."

McLure laughed. "You really think I'm smart enough to do all that?"

But Fargo kept on. "A bartender told me that you

were drunk on a boat trip back to town. You pretended to go on a fishing trip but you came back early and hid out until you could sneak out to the mansion and kill your father. A few days later you showed up so it looked like you'd been gone all that time."

"I tell you, Fargo, you sure credit me with a lot of brains I wish I had."

"Killing Bonnie was a lot easier. You waited till she went for a walk down to the boat dock. You followed her and killed her."

"A good lawyer could take all this apart in one minute. And I've got the best lawyer in the Territory."

"I guess we'll see about that, won't we?"

When they reached the jail, Fargo climbed off his horse, walked up to the buggy and told McLure to get down with his hands up. A few passersby, starting the day early, stopped walking when they saw that the man being arrested was David McLure. What the hell was going on?

Fargo took his prisoner inside. Deputy Bowers was talking to Helen Mason. She held a covered tray. Fargo could smell bacon and eggs as soon as he'd come inside.

"I'm just bringing Theo some food," Helen, dressed in a shawl over a dark dress, explained. "That café food is hard on his stomach."

Fargo looked at Bowers. "I want you to arrest McLure here. I want him in handcuffs and I want him tied to that wooden chair over there. You have guts enough to do it?"

"You try anything like that, Bowers," McLure said, "and you're through in this town. You've got a wife and three kids. Keep that in mind before you do anything foolish."

"Why are you arresting him?" Helen said.

"He's one of the killers."

"Don't let him bluff you, Bowers," McLure said. "He isn't a lawman. He's just a drifter."

"Make up your mind, Bowers," Fargo snapped.

Bowers shrugged. "You know, Mr. McLure, if I was to do what Fargo here wants me to, you rich folks would try and destroy me. But I'm running for sheriff in about three weeks and I need somethin' to set me apart from the other men who want the job." He looked down at the star on his vest. "If I arrest you now, every average voter in the town'll look up to me. I'll be the only man who took on the rich folks. I think that's going to make me damned popular."

"Go to work," Fargo said to Bowers. "I need to talk to Mason. Keep Helen here."

Bowers reached in a desk drawer and pulled out the jail keys and pitched them to Fargo.

"I won't be long," Fargo said.

Theo Mason was the jail's only occupant. The cells were as cold as the outdoors. Mason was asleep, not waking up even as Fargo made noisy work of unlocking the door.

Fargo sat on the opposite bunk and said, "Wake up, Mason." He repeated himself quickly and Mason's eyes fluttered open. He seemed disoriented for maybe twenty seconds and then he sat up on the edge of the cot.

"It's pretty damned early."

"I'm going to make this fast. I know who framed you for murder, but I can't prove it unless you tell me the truth."

"This is like a dream." He rubbed his face, then ran a hand through his mussed hair. He sure didn't look like a dandy now.

"No dream, Mason. Now get ready to tell the truth. It's the only way you're ever going to get out of this cell."

"Well," Mason said, "you sure got my attention."

A few minutes later, Fargo walked back to the front where the others were waiting.

Helen said, "This food is getting cold. I want Theo to have a warm breakfast."

"Yeah, you owe him at least some good food. But it'll take a lot of meals to make up for what you and McLure here did to him."

"What the hell are you talking about?" McLure said, his upper body fighting against the rope that lashed him to the chair.

Fargo nodded to Bowers. "Theo Mason and McLure here wanted to invest in a gold mine. They were sure it would make them rich. But neither of them could raise enough money to buy in. So they decided to embezzle money from the bank. I guess McLure figured that because it was his father's bank things would be easier. They'd planned on putting the money back when the first strike paid out. But there wasn't much gold and there was no way they could pay it back. So McLure came up with a couple more schemes and talked Mason into embezzling some more money. McLure was sure that these mines would pay off. But they didn't.

"Neither of them knew that old man McLure had secret audits done on his own—he had formal audits done to make things look right—but the secret audits were what he counted on. A few nights before he was murdered, he found out about the embezzlement. Even though he was known to be a pretty cold old man, he couldn't bring himself to prosecute his own son. He told David to take off for a week and go fishing while he thought about what to do. He couldn't get Theo arrested, either, because Theo would tell the law that David had been a part of the whole thing.

"David went fishing. But only to make it look good. He snuck back and killed his father. He used Theo's gun to do it."

"How did he get Theo's gun?" Bowers said. "That's the part that always puzzled me. It was in his desk at home."

"I thought about that, too," Fargo said. "There was only one person who could've gotten that gun for him—his mistress. Right, Helen?"

"You're insane," she snapped. She looked at Bowers. "So help me, I'll see that you're ruined for the rest of your life if you don't stop him from talking right now."

"He's startin' to make a lot of sense to me."

"Helen and McLure here have been lovers for some time, I'd expect. They could pin the whole thing on Theo because who'd believe him if he said that McLure was in on it with him? Not a man as upstanding as David McLure. They even made it look like they couldn't stand

152

each other. That argument you two had in the street sure convinced me, McLure."

He turned to Helen. "I can't say I blame you for stepping out on Theo, Helen, the way he treated you. But look at how things ended up. McLure killed his father to get one part of the estate and then he killed Bonnie to get the other part. And then he had to kill Beth because she was going to tell me everything. And now it's all falling apart."

Fargo looked over at McLure. "Killing your own flesh and blood—you think that'll come back on you when you're walking up the gallows steps? Was it hard to do? Or didn't you even think about it much?"

McLure had been quiet for a long time now. He raised his face to Fargo and said, "Like I told you, Fargo, my lawyer won't have any trouble ridiculing everything you say. And the same for Helen's lawyer."

The door opened. A gnomelike man covered in a bearskin coat came inside, stamping snow off his hand-made otter boots. He had a twisted back and a severely pocked leathery face. "Just come down from the mountains. There's a blizzard comin'. I just wondered if there's a convent around here. The nuns'll usually feed old ones like me. Maybe even give me a cot for a day or two." He looked around with glassy dark eyes. "I bet I walked in on something, didn't I?"

"I guess you did, old-timer," Fargo said. "But you can take my place and stand by the stove and get yourself warm."

"You're going?" Bowers said, sounding puzzled.

"Yeah," Fargo said. "I guess I've had just about as much of this little burg as I can handle."

"No matter where you go," McLure said, "I'll get you for this, Fargo."

Fargo nodded to Bowers. "You better take that tray back to Mason yourself, Bowers. He's not in any mood to see his wife now. I told him all about McLure and her."

"You're really going."

"I'm already gone."

The old-timer said, "But there's a blizzard comin'."

"After this town"—Fargo grinned—"a blizzard sounds almost friendly."

Five minutes later, the wind whipping up something furious, Fargo passed the TOWN LIMITS sign. If there really was a hell, it would be a lot like this little town for sure.

LOOKING FORWARD!
**The following is the opening
section of the next novel in the exciting
Trailsman series from Signet:**

**THE TRAILSMAN #312
SHANGHAIED SIX-GUNS**

*The Kingdom of Hawaii, 1861—a Garden of
Eden, but every Eden has its serpent.*

The trouble started over a woman. It often did.

Skye Fargo was having a grand time making the
rounds of the saloons and taverns along the San Francisco waterfront. His poke bulged at the seams thanks
to a lucky night at monte. Usually poker was his poison,
but in San Francisco monte was more popular, and on
a whim he had tried his hand at it and won big. Now
he was treating himself to a few days of whiskey and
sultry doves before he headed for Wyoming.

It was nice to relax, nice not to have to worry about
hostiles out to lift his hair or outlaws after his money,
or to wonder whether a hungry griz was over the next
rise or whether a rattler was in his blankets in the
morning.

As for gambling and pleasures of the flesh, neither
New Orleans nor Denver could hold a candle to San
Francisco. The city was only slightly tamer than during

its heyday of the gold rush years when, by one newspaper's estimate, there had been over five hundred saloons and taverns and almost a thousand gambling dens. Sinner's Heaven, some called it, and the nickname fit. A man could buy most anything and do most anything. The only vices frowned on were murder and rape. At one time San Francisco had a murder a night, or more, a statistic the vigilantes put a stop to by inviting those who indulged to be guests of honor at a hemp social.

San Francisco was growing up. During the day it was as respectable as any other city. But at night the lust and greed crept out of the shadows and ruled the streets and alleys until the next dawn.

It was pushing midnight when Fargo came to a seedy section of the docks and a tavern that sat off by itself near the water's edge. He almost passed the place by. But the gruff laughter and bawdy oaths that wafted from an open window, to say nothing of a particularly pleasing female voice, persuaded him to give the place a try.

Fargo paused with his hand on the latch and gazed out over the benighted bay. The water was black as pitch except for where shore lights were mirrored by the still surface. The smell of salt water and fish was strong.

Ships choked the shoreline. So many masts that in the daytime it lent the illusion of being a forest of firs. Many of the vessels, Fargo had been told, were abandoned, Gold Rush derelicts being converted to landfill as the city spread and prospered.

The hinges rasped as the door swung in. A cloud of cigar and pipe smoke wreathed Fargo. So did odors a lot less pleasant than that of the sea.

The tavern was called The Golden Gate but there was nothing golden about it. The place was as shabby and squalid an establishment as any Fargo had ever set eyes on. Lamps were few, the lighting poor, which was just as well. The floor had not been swept in a coon's age. The walls were grimy, the bar speckled with stains. So were the glasses the bartender filled and passed to customers, but no one seemed to mind.

The tavern was packed. Townsmen in high derby hats

rubbed elbows with sailors and Chinese and clean-shaven patrons of Spanish extraction who wore wide-brimmed sombreros and long serapes. Here and there were women in tight dresses with ready smiles.

One of those women attached herself to Fargo as he threaded toward the bar. A warm arm looped around his and a tantalizing violent scent eclipsed all the others. Fargo glanced into a pair of lovely eyes the same shade of blue as his. "Do you want something?" he asked with a grin.

"The name is Molly." She had curly brown hair and full lips and the tired air of a person who had seen it all and done it all, too. "Buy me a drink and I will keep you company."

"You had your choice of any gent in the place and you picked me?" Fargo asked.

"Your clothes made me curious," Molly said, plucking at one of the whangs on his sleeve. "We don't get many like you in here."

Fargo grunted. She was referring to his buckskins. His white hat, brown with dust, and his red bandanna and boots were ordinary enough, but buckskins were the mark of a frontiersman and few ever visited San Francisco.

"Don't get me wrong," Molly said. "There is nothing wrong with wearing deer hide. Hell, I don't care what a man wears so long as he is friendly and treats me nice."

"I am and I will," Fargo assured her, and sliding his arm around her slender waist, he contrived to run his hand across her bottom.

"Oh, my." Molly grinned. "Aren't you the frisky devil? But no pawing until you buy us each a drink. Otherwise I might get in trouble."

"Oh?"

"My boss doesn't like us girls to give it away for free," Molly explained. "He can be a tyrant when it comes to money."

Fargo shouldered between a pair of seamen and gave the bar a thump. "Bartender! A bottle of your best."

"You'll spoil me, handsome," Molly teased. "I'm used to the cheap stuff."

"This is just a start," Fargo said as the bottle and two dirty glasses were produced. "Later on I might treat you to a meal."

"Well, aren't you the perfect gentleman?" Molly bantered. "But Mrs. McGreagor's daughter is not one to be looking a gift horse in the mouth. Whenever you have a hankering to belly up to the feed trough, I will be honored to accompany you."

Fargo filled their glasses. He raised his and she raised hers and they clinked them together. "To your health, Molly McGreagor."

"To handsome devils in buckskins," Molly responded, and tossed her drink down with a gulp. When Fargo arched an eyebrow, she chuckled lustily and said, "I've had a lot of practice."

Motioning at their surroundings, Fargo asked, "Why this dive? You're pretty. You're bright. You could work most anywhere."

"What a kind thing to say," Molly said. "But the truth of it is, I have a temper. I have been in a few scrapes, pulled a knife a time or three, and none of the better establishments will have me."

"You don't aim to pull a knife on me, do you?" Fargo inquired, only partly in jest. Some doves were too temperamental for their own good. That, and hard drink, made them downright dangerous.

Molly laughed and touched his cheek. "Not unless you give me cause."

"Which would be what?" Fargo wanted to learn.

"I won't be laid a hand on," Molly recited. "I won't be kicked. I won't do things I don't want to do, and I expect an honest dollar for honest labor." She grinned and winked. "If you can call what I do for a living work."

Fargo decided he liked her. "Then you can rest easy. I don't beat women." The only exceptions had been females trying to kill him.

"Not all men are so considerate," Molly said. "Some are beasts. Oh, they smile and treat a girl nice until they get her in the bedroom. But once the door is locked and the shades are down they turn into brutes. I have a friend by the name of Claire who had all her teeth knocked out. Another friend had her cheek cut and is scarred for life." Molly grew serious and grim. "That's not for me, thank you very much. I have too much pride to let anyone abuse me."

Fargo refilled her glass.

"If you ask me, there is too much wickedness in the world," Molly declared. "The older I get, the more it bothers me. Silly, I suppose, but a person can't help how they feel." She nudged his arm. "How about you?"

"I feel like getting you under the sheets," Fargo said.

Molly blinked, then laughed. Upending her glass, she drained it and smacked it down on the bar. "Point taken. I apologize. I am here to show you a good time, not to prattle on so."

Before Fargo could tell her that was not what he meant, he was jostled from behind. A blow so hard he was knocked against the bar and spilled some of his drink. As he started to turn, a man bellowed in anger.

"Consarn it! Watch where you're goin', missy! You damn near made me drop my grog!"

Fargo was not the only man who had been bumped. Two others were straightening and a third dripped with spilled liquor. What made it all the more remarkable was the party responsible.

It was a woman. Not much more than five feet tall, she was hidden in the folds of a woolen cloak and hood. Only her lustrous raven hair was visible, spilling as it did from out of the hood. The cloak was too long and dragged on the floor; plainly it was not hers but belonged to someone bigger. She looked up at them, her face lost in the folds of the hood, and said in oddly accented English, "I am sorry. I did not mean to disturb you."

The townsman with the liquor on his clothes was not satisfied. "What you meant be hanged, girl! My glass was practically full! You owe me the price of a drink."

The woman in the cloak did not say anything. Her hood swiveled toward the entrance and back again.

"Didn't you hear me?" the townsman demanded. "You owe me. Pay up." He held out his hand.

"I do not have money," the black-haired mystery woman said. "Again, I am very sorry." She sounded sincere.

"Sorry doesn't wet my throat." The townsman, a broomstick in a bowler hat, grabbed her arm.

Fargo was set to intervene but Molly beat him to it.

"You heard the girl, Stanley. Let her go. Accidents happen."

"Stay out of this, Molly," Stanley snapped. "You're not the one whose clothes need washing."

"Since when do you make a fuss over a little spilled red-eye?" Molly demanded. "When you are in your cups you can't hardly hold your drinks steady."

Stanley was not amused. "All I am saying is this girl owes me for what she made me spill. She must make good."

The woman in the cloak tried to pull free. "I have already told you I do not have money."

"Then maybe you can repay me in another way." Leering, Stanley pulled her close and tried to push her hood back but she slapped his wrist away. "Here now, girl! None of that. You're about to make me mad."

Molly stepped past Fargo and pried at the man's long fingers. "Pretend you have manners, Stan, and release her."

Without warning, Stanley gave Molly a shove that sent her stumbling against Fargo. "Enough of this! I won't have a saloon tart tell me what I should and should not do."

Flushing with anger, Molly raised her hand to slap him. Fargo made no attempt to stop her. He was half tempted to slug the jackass himself.

But just then a pair of sailors shouldered through the press of patrons and halted on either side of the woman in the cloak. One of the sailors was tall and lanky, the other of medium height and as broad as a brick wall. They ignored Stanley and Molly. Seizing the mystery woman's wrist, the tall sailor said, "We've caught up to you at last, little one. You thought you were clever but here we are."

Their quarry had stiffened and gasped. She sought to pull free but the tall sailor would not let go.

"No, you don't. We had to chase you all over creation town and you are not getting away as easy as that."

"Let's cart her back," said the human wall. "The captain is mad enough and will only get madder the longer we take."

Fargo was as surprised as Molly, who stood with her luscious mouth gaping wide. Not so Stanley, who placed a hand on the tall sailor's shoulder and said, "Hold on there, friend. If this woman is a friend of yours, she owes me for a drink."

"What are you babbling about? Unhand me," the tall sailor said, and cuffed the townsman across the face.

Stanley staggered against the bar, his glass shattering on the floorboards at his feet. Everyone within ten feet heard the crack of the slap and stopped whatever they were doing to turn and stare. Fights were all too common in dives like this, and were a prime source of entertainment.

The sailors went to leave. The tall one started to haul the woman in the cloak after him but Stanley howled in outrage and darted around in front of them.

"Not so fast, damn your bones! You can't go around slapping people and get away with it."

Fargo wanted no part of their squabble. He was there for a good time, and only a good time. He was curious about the woman in the cloak but that was as far as his interest went. Then the woman wrenched loose of the tall sailor and clutched at his buckskins.

"Please help me," she pleaded, her features lost in the folds of her hood. "They are holding me against my will."

"None of that, bitch," the tall sailor said. "Cause us trouble and the captain will take a switch to you." He snatched at her cloak.

She ducked and his fingers snagged her hood. Out spilled her luxurious mane of thick black hair, framing an exotic oval face with beautiful dark eyes. There was fear in those eyes, fear and an eloquent appeal.

"Oh, hell," Fargo said. He unleashed an uppercut that caught the tall sailor on the point of his chin and crumpled him like so much paper.

Stanley picked that moment to take a swing at the other sailor. He missed. The sailor then threw a punch at Stanley and hit another man instead, who fell against others. The next moment it seemed like everyone was pushing and shoving and cursing and swinging.

Molly leaned toward Fargo and yelled in his ear, "We have to get her out of here!" She pushed him toward the end of the bar and a side door he had not noticed. "That way!" Taking the other woman's hand, Molly led the way, staying close to the bar, which most of the men had abandoned to take gleeful part in the brawl.

Fargo did not need prompting. The last thing he wanted was to be caught up in a tavern fight. If things got out of hand the city police were bound to show up, and they were notorious for busting heads and sorting out the culprits later. But he had taken only a couple of steps when a rough hand fell on his shoulder and he was spun around.

"Hand the girl over!" the muscular sailor snarled, and brandished a knife.

No other series packs this much heat!

THE TRAILSMAN

#294: OREGON OUTLAWS
#295: OASIS OF BLOOD
#296: SIX-GUN PERSUASION
#297: SOUTH TEXAS SLAUGHTER
#298: DEAD MAN'S BOUNTY
#299: DAKOTA DANGER
#300: BACKWOODS BLOODBATH
#301: HIGH PLAINS GRIFTERS
#302: BLACK ROCK PASS
#303: TERROR TRACKDOWN
#304: DEATH VALLEY DEMONS
#305: WYOMING WIPEOUT
#306: NEBRASKA NIGHT RIDERS
#307: MONTANA MARAUDERS
#308: BORDER BRAVADOS
#309: CALIFORNIA CARNAGE
#310: ALASKAN VENGEANCE

TRAILSMAN GIANT: IDAHO BLOOD SPOOR

**Available wherever books are sold or at
penguin.com**

"A writer in the tradition of Louis L'Amour
and Zane Grey!"
—*Huntsville Times*

National Bestselling Author
RALPH COMPTON

NOWHERE, TEXAS
THE SKELETON LODE
DEATH RIDES A CHESNUT MARE
WHISKEY RIVER
TRAIN TO DURANGO
DEVIL'S CANYON
SIX GUNS AND DOUBLE EAGLES
THE BORDER EMPIRE
AUTUMN OF THE GUN
THE KILLING SEASON
THE DAWN OF FURY
DEATH ALONG THE CIMMARON
RIDERS OF JUDGMENT
BULLET CREEK
FOR THE BRAND
GUNS OF THE CANYONLANDS
BY THE HORNS
THE TENDERFOOT TRAIL
RIO LARGO
DEADWOOD GULCH
A WOLF IN THE FOLD
TRAIL TO COTTONWOOD FALLS
BLUFF CITY

Available wherever books are sold or at
penguin.com

SIGNET

Another thrilling tale from
Charles G. West

OUTLAW

SOME MEN CHOSE TO LIVE
OUTSIDE THE LAW.

Matt Slaughter and his older brother joined the
Confederacy only when war came to the
Shenandoah Valley. But with the cause lost, they
desert for home—only to find that swindlers
have taken their farm. When his brother
accidentally kills a Union officer, Matt takes the
blame. Facing a sham trial and a noose, he
escapes to the West, living as an outlaw who
neither kills for pleasure nor steals for profit.
But there are other men who are
cold-blooded and have no such scruples...

<u>Also Available</u>:
Vengeance Moon
The Hostile Trail

Available wherever books are sold or at
penguin.com